T0065037

TEXAS
SUMMER

TEXAS SUMMER

A NOVEL BY

TERRY SOUTHERN

PREFACE BY RIP TORN

ARCADE PUBLISHING / *New York*

First Skyhorse edition

Arcade Publishing books may be purchased in bulk at special discounts for sales promotion, corporate gifts, fund-raising, or educational purposes. Special editions can also be created to specifications. For details, contact the Special Sales Department, Arcade Publishing, 307 West 36th Street, 11th Floor, New York, NY 10018 or arcade@skyhorsepublishing.com.

Arcade Publishing® is a registered trademark of Skyhorse Publishing, Inc.®, a Delaware corporation.

Visit our website at www.arcadepub.com.

10 9 8 7 6 5 4 3 2 1

Library of Congress Cataloging-in-Publication Data is available on file.

Cover painting and design © 1992 by Wendell Minor

Print ISBN: 978-1-62872-433-2

Printed in the United States of America

For Gail

PREFACE
by Rip Torn

I met Terry on the film *The Cincinnati Kid* in 1967, and we became friends. I used to visit him and his longtime companion, Gail Gerber, in Canaan, Connecticut — with my wife at the time, Geraldine Page, and our three children. Terry had created an oasis for himself on his farm, a beautiful eighteenth-century house which had belonged to Samuel Forbes, with plenty of acreage. Gail was a former movie actress, ballet dancer, and teacher, a great cook and lots of fun. Arriving at night was magical. They'd have fires roaring inside, and outside were candles in various outdoor colored-glass sconces. I'm a longtime gardener, and I was very impressed by Mr. Edward Ustico, their Italian neighbor and plumber, who used to cut the fields with a sickle. He grew tomatoes from Italian seeds that were the best I ever tasted.

The farm was a great place for his son, Nile, and Terry raised him in a "classic-Texan" manner, teaching him to shoot, hunt, and fish. Terry always had a number of dogs on the farm, and they'd run like mad up and down the banks of the Blackberry River—barreling into the house wet and stinking. Sometimes they'd have porcupine quills in their mouths—which Terry took out using pliers.

Terry asked me to help him teach his son to shoot clay pigeons (skeet), and I remember the three of us in the great field in front of the house—Terry with his .12 gauge (the biggest shotgun made), me with a .20 gauge, and Nile with a "ladies gun"—an under-and-over double-barreled .410. By the end of the day, Nile was shooting two birds on one pull! Terry also asked me to teach Nile to hunt deer, I think because he felt it was easier to learn from someone other than your father. As a boy from Texas, my grandfather taught me, and Terry's uncle had taught him. I could tell Nile was a bit nervous, not only about the size of the game but about being out with me instead of his dad. We walked through the beautiful Berkshire open fields towards where we could see some bucks feeding in the distance. Though we had on our diversionary scents, we were still upwind— which is the worst place to be—and after a little breeze, they were tipped off. It was just as well, as I could tell Nile was keen to get back to the farm. When Terry insisted I take Nile out again, I told him, "That boy does something I'd never do—he likes to *run with the dogs*—it's sensational! And dangerous as hell—he's got no *fear* whatsoever. . . . So, let him run with the dogs!" There was no more talk of deer hunting.

I'm from Temple, Texas, and I think Terry, because he had a refined, eloquent way of speaking, thought I didn't believe he was Texan. He used to show me photographs of his family's home in Alvarado, shaking his head in something like his own disbelief. I never doubted it, especially when he reverted to his Texan drawl—which was always funny. "Ah'll tell you one thang," he'd say, or, "Got-dang!"

I've known and worked with a lot of writers over the years: Norman Mailer, James Baldwin, and Jack Gelber: They all put Terry at #1—describing his writing as "monumental," "profound," and, as Norman said, "cool, mean, and deliberate."

Terry wrote many fantastic screenplays, among them *Easy Rider*. His pacing, sense of character, empathy with regular folk, and feeling for the way country people talk come through in that movie with as much clarity and sense of place as they do in *Texas Summer*.

I miss Terry—he was my bud!

TEXAS
SUMMER

I

T EXAS SUMMER MORNING, the softly bleak hour after dawn, the boy Harold and his father slowly hunted across a vast scrub-brush tumbleweed field, toward a mist-seeping river-bottom grove in the middle distance — Harold, at twelve, carrying his old single-shot twenty, and his father the twelve-gauge double with the Magnum-load.

Moving a few feet ahead of them, a shoot of Johnson grass in his mouth, dangled there, shifting it from one side to the other in his own ultra-blasé fashion, was C.K., the twenty-three-year-old black who worked for Harold's father. Ahead of C.K., and ranging out on either side, were the two bird dogs, Red and Ring — an Irish setter and a short-haired hound of more obscure lineage.

C.K. maintained a soft unbroken flow of conversation with the two dogs that was mostly incomprehensible, except of course, presumably, to the dogs themselves. Steady and rhythmic, it was at times almost hypnotic: ". . . *look out now . . . git on it, Ring . . . pick it up, Red . . . study the bird . . . look out now . . . that's right . . . you got it, Red . . . look out now . . .*"

Suddenly, the red setter froze, on point, an oil painting, while the black-and-tan, looking the other way, failed to pick it up and continued ahead, sniffing the ground from side to side.

"Red got 'im," said C.K. in hushed urgency to the other dog, *"quit it, Ring . . ."*

At that instant, two quail burst from the bramble cover as if they had been blown out of it. Both guns came up together and three shots roared almost as one. The nearest bird dropped straight down, in an oddly unreal way, as though it had been suspended by a wire, abruptly snapped — but the second one veered crazily to the right, then down in a fluttering spiral, and the dogs looked on with what appeared to be genuine interest and curiosity before rushing forward to find the birds.

"Meat-on-the-table," murmured C.K., less in anticipation than habit, as he followed the dogs.

"I think you got that second one, Son," said Harold's father, not looking at him as he reloaded.

Harold said nothing, and dropped a shell into the chamber of his single-shot.

His father snapped shut the twelve-gauge. "Ain't that right, C.K.? Didn't it look to you like he brought down that second bird?"

"Aw you got both of 'em," said Harold. "No use makin' him lie about it."

"I didn't hear you, C.K.," his father persisted, tilting his head, waiting for the right words.

C.K. spoke without looking. "Well now, ah cain't rightly say. . . . C'mere, Ring. . . . Ah knowed that he come up too late on this here one — gimme the bird, Red — but he might of got a piece of the second."

Harold sighed in exasperation. "He got 'em both, an' you know it."

C.K., undaunted, already smoothing the feathers of the dead quail in his hand, half closed his eyes and spoke with softly labored patience: "Well now, like ah say, ah cain't rightly be sure 'bout that second bird, 'cause ah wudn't studyin' that second bird — you unnerstan' what ah mean, ah had my eye on the fust one." Finally flicking his expressionless gaze past Harold, he took the other bird from the dog's mouth. "These here are good young birds," he observed. "Nice and plump."

Harold glared at him. "Uh-huh. Well, I'd sure hate for my life to depend on how good you can lie."

His father frowned at him. "Now, boy," he said severely, "you got no call to talk to C.K. like that. An' I don't want to hear it again, you understand?"

Harold's mouth set as he looked away from his father, who then demanded: "Well, do you?"

"Yessir," Harold mumbled in his most perfunctory manner.

Satisfied, his father looked toward the eastern sky, the red light there feathering up through the gray dawn, slowly bleeding across the whole endless Texas horizon.

"Well, I reckon these will do us," he said. "Let's head on back to the house . . . 'fore the biscuits git cold."

And as the three of them turned to go — Harold's father in front — C.K. caught Harold's eye and, with only the faintest smile on his face, gave him a wink.

II

A BLAZING AFTERNOON, Harold and C.K. worked to repair a break in the barbed-wire pasture fence. Without shirts, they sweated under the terrible sun, C.K. wearing an old straw hat and a pair of worn-out rawhide gloves. They worked in silence, C.K. kneeling to use the wire-stretcher on the bottom strand, and telling Harold when to place one of the heavy wire-staples that the boy was carrying in his mouth, point-ends out.

"That be fine, Hal," C.K. said, "hold it right there." "Hal" was not a nickname but the way C.K. pronounced "Harold."

The boy placed one of the staples over the wire, and C.K. hammered it in.

"Best use two," he said then. "This old locus' wood done begin to rot out on us."

"How old is it?" Harold wanted to know.

"This wood post? Oh it mighty old awright, likely older'n you and me put together. See, this here is *black* locus' wood. They reckon that the hardest wood they is."

Drawing away from the fence after C.K. started nailing

6

the second staple, Harold brushed the back of his hand against one of the double-pronged barbs of the wire.

"Dang!" He dropped the staples from his mouth into his right hand and licked the back of his left.

"You snag you hand?" C.K. asked. "Lemme see," and he examined it. "Ah done told you to wear you gloves, din't ah? 'Always wear gloves when you work with bob-wire n' bramble' — that's gospel, anybody tell you that . . . but you hand be awright, that wire ain't rust out yet. Jest lick it again." He took off his left glove and tossed it to Harold. "Here, we each use one of these."

Harold muttered something just short of thanks, putting the staples back in his mouth.

"An ah tell you somethin' else," said C.K., "long as ah set up here in the free ad-vice business. You shouldn't talk with them hook-nails in you mouth. Fact is, you shouldn't put 'em in you mouth noways."

"I ain't gonna swaller none," said Harold, and added for good measure: "You must be crazy."

"Uh-huh. You try sayin that when you got one caught down in you throat like a big ole fishhook! Hee-hee! Then you go, 'Aaaacch . . . aaacch . . .' " He did a comic grotesquerie of someone choking to death, falling back on the ground, gasping, clutching his throat, eyes rolling, legs kicking, playing the fool.

Harold had to laugh at the outlandish spectacle, and in doing so, nearly swallowed one of the staples.

He spat them all out in a fit. "Dang you, C.K.! I nearly did swaller one of 'em! 'Cause of you carryin on like a dang idiot!"

"Wal, maybe now you take serious what I say."

He helped Harold, who was still muttering accusations,

find the staples he had spit onto the ground. "Shoot," he said then, "you know what? All this talk 'bout fishhook put me in mind of that big ole bullhead catfish. Maybe we oughtta mosey on down to the tank and git him on a stringer."

The idea was not without its appeal to Harold. "I turned up some bloodworms this mornin'," he said, "right next to that old hog-trough — they was big as grass-snakes! Heck, I bet they're still there."

C.K. hung the wire-stretcher on the top strand of the fence and brushed his hands. "Shoot," he said, squinting up at the sun, "that's jest what that catfish go for 'bout now . . . big ole fat juicy bloodworm."

With their poles and their worms, they started across a pasture, down toward the water tank. Scattered about the pasture were six or seven cows and, much farther away, one very large bull. When they were about halfway across, the bull raised its head and stared at them.

"Look at that," said Harold, "there's that dang ole red bull . . . lookin' straight at us."

C.K. laughed. "Uh-huh . . . an' lookin' mean too, ain't he?"

"He *is* mean. And you know it."

"You ain't scared none though, is you, Hal?"

Harold chuckled. "Scared of a mean bull? I guess you're gonna say you ain't."

C.K. shifted the stem of grass in his mouth, laid his head back, eyes closed, blasé-style. "Ah ain't scared of nothin' that ah knows how to handle."

"Shoot, you're crazy. Besides, how can you handle a mean bull?"

"Well, ah tell you how — that red bull come at me right now, you know how ah do?"

"Run like all dang get-out, that's how you'd do."

C.K. shook his head. "Uh-uh. Oh no. Ah stan' my ground . . . ah wait till he close" — he pointed — "like right up to that mesquite bush, then ah quick-step to the side" — he executed an exaggerated matador movement — "like that, you see, an' that bull jest go right by me."

Harold stared at him for a moment. "Shoot," he said, "that's the biggest dang lie I ever heard."

About fifty yards away, the bull, still staring fixedly at them, slowly pawed the ground with one front hoof, then lowered his head . . . and resumed grazing, at the same time moving off, unhurriedly, in the opposite direction. Both had watched him, but neither spoke, until C.K. said: "Want me to git him over here an' show you how ah do?"

Harold scoffed. "Is that how come you waited till he was headed the other way?"

"Ah bet ah still git him — you want me to try?"

Feeling the blood rise along his spine, Harold looked at the distance to the nearest fence, calculating the risk.

"Sure," he said, trying to sound calm, "go ahead."

"Okay, now you watch how ah git 'im ovah," said C.K., "an' then how ah do." He began clapping his hands and jumping up and down. "You! Red Bull!" he yelled. "Come on! Come on! Come git me! You ole Red! Come on!"

He danced around crazily, waving both arms and his fishing pole over his head.

The bull stopped grazing and looked up, regarding him curiously.

"*Come on, Red!*" C.K. continued at the top of his voice. "*Come on, you ugly ole Red!*"

The bull raised his head higher, and then, quite suddenly, began trotting toward them, slowly at first, head still high, almost doglike in its strangely alert and inquisitive manner . . . while C.K. kept at it, cavorting about, carrying on, playing the fool, though at the same time now eyeing the fence line and angling toward it, with Harold alongside, when the trotting changed, as though in a shift of gears, into a gallop, and now the bull was charging full tilt, his approach an awesome rumble. Harold and C.K. tried briefly to outwait each other before breaking into a run, as they finally did, more or less at the same time, and just slightly before the last available moment.

And then they were in all-out and ludicrous flight to the fence, hurling their poles ahead of them over it and scrambling after, tumbling in a heap on the other side, gasping and laughing — while the great bull stood behind the wire, head down, the brass ring in its nose glittering in the afternoon sun, eyes glowering, nostrils flared and snorting, front hooves pawing the ground as though preparing a foothold for a monumental charge through the taut four-wire fence itself.

"God dang," said Harold softly, sitting up, breathless and excited, "he sure can run, can't he?"

C.K. tried to be more restrained in his assessment. "Uh-huh, well, you seen how ah don't take no chance, how ah done cal-culate jest how close he be to us, an' us to the fence, you see what ah mean?"

"Oh sure," said Harold sarcastically, "an' I seen that quick-step you was gonna use, too. That was some quick-step you used. Ha."

Just beyond the fence, head low, the bull still glowered.

"Look at that red bull!" exclaimed Harold, slightly in

awe. "He's jest about ready to tear through that dang bob-wire."

"Naw he ain't," said C.K., waxing expansive as he stood up and leisurely brushed himself off, head back, eyes half-closed. "He all bluff. He ain't mess with us again — now he knows ah onto his move." He leaned over and adroitly swooped up another piece of Johnson grass to chew at the jaunty angle, while Harold, still sitting on the ground, could only gaze up at him, mouth slightly agape in dumb wonder at the enormity of the lie.

C.K. looked down with a frown of mock severity.

"Well, saddle up, my man," he said then, smiling and extending a hand to help Harold to his feet. "Let's head on down to the tank an' git that ole catfish in the skillet!"

The half-acre pond, or tank, as it was known, was about one-third the size of a football field, and was surrounded by weeping willows. It had been dug out by shovel and a mule-drawn plow, many years ago, by Harold's grand-father and a hired hand — after consultation with the dowser woman, Willow Wanda, whom they referred to as "Willer Wander" or, sometimes, "the Dowsin' Demon." Now long dead, she was still remembered and talked about through-out the county. An ancient crone of indeterminate lineage, she was toothless, crippled, and smelled of strange oint-ments. Sometimes she claimed to be a "Gypsy dancer," but others said she was a half-breed Comanche who had been cast out of her tribe. Frowned upon by men, loathed by women, feared and taunted by children — yet it would have been deemed the ultimate folly to dig into the parched red earth of Johnson County in search of water without the ad-vice and sanction of "Demon Willer."

Closed-eyed, she would traverse the general area where the water was needed, hobbling grotesquely, dribbling saliva from her thin lips as they trembled in the "unknown tongue" — in which she appeared to be proficient, both at work in the field and in her devotion at the Tabernacle of the Seventh Seal, the Holy Roller church of her persuasion. People who had seen her in action would recount how the willow branch, with which she divined the location of the subterranean stream, would fly toward the ground with such force that it would sometimes cause a red welt on her ankle, should it strike there instead of the earth.

"Did you ever see that dang old dowser woman?" Harold asked now, as they came in view of the pond — or at least the tops of the willows around it. "The one that planted the first of them willers."

C.K. gave him a frown of surprise. "Who, the ole Dowsin' Demon? Why she be dead an' gone long 'fore ah git heah, Hal — you oughtta know that."

"Oh," said Harold, mildly chagrined. "I guess I wudn't thinkin' . . ."

He fell silent, but C.K., as if not wanting to disappoint the boy, went on in a cheerful tone: "But ah tell you who ah did see onct — was that ole Wander's *pro*-jay."

"Her what?"

"Her pro-jay."

"What the heck is that?"

"Well now, you see, 'pro-jay' is what they call somebody who try to be somebody else."

"How could they do that?" Harold wanted to know.

"Well, they study his moves, you see . . . an' they listen to what he say . . . an' they try to do like he do . . . so they's called the 'pro-jay' — that's what they's called. Like

take me'n you now, goin' fishin', you be my pro-jay at fishin'
. . . other things too."

Harold frowned. "Like what?"

"Oh" — C.K. smiled up at the summer sky, feeling sublime in his infinite richness of choice — "like stringin' fence
wire."

"Uh-huh," said Harold, "well, I'll tell you one thing —
I'm sure glad you didn't say 'bullfightin.' Ha."

But C.K. was not the flappable kind. "Oh that red bull
knowed when he beat — ah respect him for that — he seed
how ah was onto his move."

Harold scoffed. "Yeah, well I seen how you move, too
— I seen you head for tall cotton!"

C.K. laid his head back with a sigh of exasperation, eyes
half-closed as though in suffering. "What you seed," he explained, "was my *'sponsibility* . . . my *'sponsibility in action*
— that's what you seed. 'Cause when ah knows they was
a chance of you gittin' hurt by that bull, that's when ah put
my move on — you see what ah mean?"

"Oh sure," said Harold, now pretending to have lost all
interest.

"But like ah say," C.K. prattled on, "ah seen this ole woman
who claim she the pro-jay of the Dowsin' Demon. She a white
woman, but she come to the colored-people church, an' she
be touched an' speak in the unknown tongue . . . fack be,
she claim she in di-rect descent from Willer Wander."

As was often the case, Harold found himself half wondering if C.K. might not be making up the whole thing,
and from the side he watched his face with suspicion. At
times like these, C.K., aware of his listener's skepticism,
might venture a remark to reassure credulity — or, for mischievous reasons of his own, to magnify disbelief.

" 'Course ah never seen her dowse," he went on, "but they say she mighty good, they say she never miss, eben in red-dirt."

"Shoot," said Harold, and he was about to comment further, but C.K. suddenly gestured caution with his hand, staring intently ahead, face tilted to one side, as in an odd attitude of listening, and his eyes slightly wild. "Let's jest ease up now," he said softly. "Ah don't want that bullhead know we comin'."

Harold shot him a quick look. "I reckon you think he *can* see us. Ha. I guess you really *are* crazy after all."

"That ole bullhead know more than you think he do," said C.K., moving carefully to his left, still keeping his eyes toward the pond. "How come you think he git to be so old an' so big? Shoot, that fish know more'n me an' you put together 'bout some things."

"Yeah, like what?" the boy demanded, following C.K., and keeping his voice down, just in case.

"Like when a grasshopper got a fishhook in it."

"Huh?"

C.K. nodded sagely. "That how smart Mistuh Bullhead be — if they two grasshopper kickin' roun' in the water, an' one of 'em got fishhook in it, ready to snag that bullhead, right away bullhead know which one, an' he don't mess with it, he go for the one without no hook."

"Sure," said Harold, more to argue than agree, "that's because a grasshopper with a fishhook stuck through it ain't gonna move like a regular grasshopper — it's gonna be all jerkin' round. Anybody knows that."

C.K. sighed in closed-eyed exasperation. "Ah talkin' 'bout when you *mash* the other grasshopper — like twist it in the middle, so it be all jerky and kickin' round, too, jest like the one with the hook in it — that bullhead still know the difference."

Harold stared at him for a moment. "Uh-huh, then how we ever gonna catch 'im?"

"We outsmart him, that's how . . . we *sur*-prise him. He don't know we here he won't 'spect no fishhook."

The pond was like an oasis in a desert, a Shangri-la, with an atmosphere, almost a climate, separate from its immediate surroundings. A shimmering oval of crystalline blue, fringed with weeping willows interwoven in a soft-focus double ring because of their reflection in the water, the pond resembled an exotic blue mirror, its frame intricately filigreed. But there was something else — something curiously, classically, of Texas about the scene — a quality of strange hidden contrasts, something of abrupt mystery . . . a secret celebration of nature at its most darkly persuasive: the diamondback rattler coiled in a field of bluebonnets, the scorpion beneath the yellow rose.

Quietly now, and at C.K.'s indication, they settled down on the bank near one side of a huge uprooted cottonwood. Its giant trunk jutted up about ten feet out of the water, at an unnatural and challenging angle, sinister in its suggestion of the violence that could have brought it to such a grotesque end.

"This jest where ole bullhead be 'bout now," said C.K. softly, as he threaded a large, writhing bloodworm onto a big number-2 hook, and Harold did the same, though with somewhat less conviction.

He finished baiting his hook and looked at C.K. "An' I suppose he ain't gonna notice these worms got hooks in 'em."

C.K. didn't reply, concentrating instead on his own handiwork, intent and fastidious, as if preparing an exquisite trout-fly for a fisherman-king. And finally, with equal deliberateness, and a show of vague reverence, he carefully spat on it, before swinging it out to an exact place in the water, about a foot from the cottonwood log. Only then did he inspect Harold's baited hook, fingering it gingerly. "He gonna notice *this* one got hook in it," he said. "Fack is, he may steal this bait, the way you got it on all lopside. Then he be onto us, an' we say, 'good-bye, Mistuh Bull-head!' Lemme fix it, you keep eye on my line."

And while C.K. rearranged his bait, Harold watched the bobber on C.K.'s line — an ordinary bottle-cork split up the side — how it lay on the still water, absolutely without movement, while the line, visible just below the surface, trailed off and disappeared into the depths beneath the great log itself.

"Don't try an' snag 'im," C.K. cautioned, "till the cork go all the way under."

Harold scoffed. "Are you crazy? Don't you think I know how to fish? I probably fished as much as you have — maybe more."

C.K. nodded. "Uh-huh. But you ain't study it. Like with this bullhead . . . Now you see the way ah put that worm right down to the end of the hook? . . . Well, bullhead got to take that hook-point 'fore he get *any* you worm. That way you set you hook, when you jerk up, you snag his jaw — that call 'set the hook' — you know what ah say?"

"Well, everybody knows that, dang it," said Harold. "What's wrong with you?"

Although its existence was a matter of common knowledge, neither Harold nor C.K. had actually ever gotten a good look at the giant catfish — except that once when Harold and his friend Big Lawrence had been fooling around

at the pond, taking a fruit-jar crammed with fireflies (or
"ligh'nin'-bugs" as they called them) and had pushed the
sealed jar as far under the water as they could to see what
would happen. ("Them bugs are all full of *phosphrus*," Lawrence had explained. "The pressure will make 'em blow up!")
Harold was gazing down past the jar of pulsating light, and
he had seen it — not recognizable at first — resting on the
dark bottom: something so big and so still that he thought
it was an unfamiliar rock, or a sunken log, like a heavy three-
foot piece of firewood. But one part of him must have
guessed what it really was, because he continued to stare
. . . beyond the magic lantern of fireflies, mesmerized by
the thing that lay beneath it — motionless (or was it?) —
in the eerie strobelike swatch of hypnotic light. And then
the rock, log, whatever it was, had slowly begun to drift
along the bottom, toward the shadowy depths beyond, and
finally into them, as though to be obscured forever. ("*God
dang* . . . ," Harold had whispered, realizing what it was,
with a gradual shock that had made the back of his neck
tingle.) And when he told Big Lawrence that he had just
seen the legendary monster-fish, Lawrence seemed to believe him, but said he thought he was "lyin' 'bout how dang
big it was" — so they had gotten into a fight about that,
and Big Lawrence had won, but not before getting a front
tooth knocked into his upper lip, which had bled with un-
due profusion so that one sleeve of his shirt was covered
with blood from his wiping his mouth on it. But then, instead of trying to wash it out in the pond, he'd let the blood
dry on his sleeve and made up a story about how he and
Harold had "got jumped by some Mex'cans, an' one of 'em
pulled a knife on us." In telling this to Tommy Sellers and
Ralph Newgate, Big Lawrence added: "Reckon he won't

be pullin' a knife on nobody else right soon!" then grinned crazily and nodded at Harold for confirmation. But Harold had just looked away, and said later: "Heck, I ain't gonna back you in a dang lie — not after us gettin' into it over you callin' *me* one."

But regarding the existence of the great fish, there were witnesses to prove it. Harold's Uncle Buck, on his mother's side — an angler of such excellence and repute that he was habitually entered, and often highly placed, in "The Famous Lake Mead's Big Texas Bass Tournament" — had driven over from Amarillo one Sunday and spent the entire next week trying to land the big fish, which he hooked three different times — with a loss of lures, lines, rods, and specially prepared flies. "Wal, ah'll tell you *one* thing," he had said in conclusion, over the chicken and dressing, hot biscuits, and giblet gravy at Sunday dinner before heading back for Amarillo. "That bullhead is a smart son'bitch!" He told how the hooked fish would burst up through the surface, raging and thrashing to a height of four or five feet above the water, then dive into the depths, head for the nearest stump, wrap around it, and snap the line. A proud and ethical fisherman, who preferred to play the fish, exhaust it, and outsmart it, he had begun by using a four-pound test line and a feather-light bamboo rod, then had gradually moved up to thirty-pound test and a rod made of some kind of new alloy. "Ah ever go after him again," he said, unsmiling, at the dinner table, "it'll be with a length of calf-rope or a goddam dog-chain."

When Harold had first told C.K. about seeing the great bullhead, C.K. had not doubted the fact, nor even questioned the size; instead he nodded solemnly and said: "He be back — we git 'im." That was two years ago, and they had not seen the fish since — although both Uncle Buck and Harold's grandfather had hooked it, on separate occasions, the latter as recently as two months ago. "Felt like I had a goddam hog on the line," he had insisted, "and then he hit them stumps, and it was 'Katy, bar the door!' Snapped my rod, snapped my line, and that was all she wrote! Damnest thing I ever seen!"

"Ah got me a feelin'," said C.K. somberly now, as they gazed at the motionless split-corks floating on the water in front of them, about a foot apart.

Harold gave him a skeptical glance. "Oh yeah? What kind of feelin'?"

C.K. frowned. "Well, it ain't that easy to say, but it's like what you might call a church feelin' — like somethin' you might feel just 'fore you git 'teched.' "

"Are you crazy? Since when did you ever go to church?"

But as C.K. prepared to expound on it, a remarkable thing happened: both corks began to move slowly toward them across the water — for about six inches before they were jerked under the surface, with such abruptness as to cause wide concentric circles to ripple out across the pond.

"God dang," said Harold, "that must be him!"

"Snag up!" C.K. yelled. "Snag up, he done took both hook!"

Almost simultaneously the two rods bent into hairpin shape, and the reels spun with a high singing whine as the lines unspooled.

"Let out!" yelled C.K., quite needlessly. "Play the fish! Play the fish!"

But there was to be no playing this fish; it had taken both baits in one wide-mouth sweeping rush, and when it felt the resistance of the two hooks, caught now between gill and the thick bone of its lower jaw, it went berserk. Turning, twisting, writhing, the great bullhead raged along the bottom — between rock, log, and clump of cattail reed, its body contorting crazily, like a kind of torpedo gone haywire.

"He's headin' for the stump!" yelled C.K., as both their lines whined wildly out of the reels and snapped taut and quivering like two bowstrings.

C.K. was now performing a veritable tarantella of panic. "Reel in!" he shrieked. "Reel in!"

"The lines are gonna break off if we do," said Harold grimly — but they tried it. As for the great fish below, this abrupt and unexpected double tug of restraint drove its fury beyond all tolerance. It seemed to shake its head — like a horse or bull — preparing for a monumental desperate maneuver, which it then executed: pushing off from the bottom with the lower half of its body, it was thrust upward with the propulsion of a dolphin, and it slashed through the still surface of the water, this giant catfish, rising five or six feet above the geyser-churned surface, its body convulsed in shuddering rage. Then, for an instant, it appeared to be suspended in midair, its full length arched like a bucking horse.

On the bank Harold and C.K. could only stand and watch in stone wonder — not so much at the great size of the fish, but at something much more remarkable: like Ahab's whale, its body was festooned, from gill to tail, with bits of glistening nylon line, hooks, lures, spinners, and trout-flies — many of them rusted dull to be sure, but enough of them enameled and still red-devil bright, some bejeweled, gold and silver, historic trinkets that caught the fading rays of the sun in a breathtaking spangle of multicolored light.

"*Lawd, lawd . . . ,*" whispered C.K.

Then it plummeted — headfirst, again like a dolphin, except for its convulsed writhing — and, as Harold and C.K. plainly saw, seemingly even before it hit the water, it headed for the stumps. Their lines, now quivering with tension a foot above the water, were hopelessly crisscrossed as the fish zigzagged crazily through the maze of stumps, wrapping the lines around one, then another, causing both lines — in their length between rod and the first stump — to go suddenly, sickeningly, slack.

C.K. sighed with great weariness. "Oh mercy, mercy . . . ," he murmured softly, and he started reeling in his severed line. Harold did likewise.

"Maybe he's hung up out there on one of them stumps," the boy suggested hopefully.

"Nope," C.K. said flatly, "he is long gone."

And at that instant, as if to verify his observation, on the other side of the pond, in a swatch of sunlight well beyond the stumps, there was a sudden swirl and a widening circle of ripples, at the center of which was momentarily visible not only the dark form of the fish itself, but the small cluster of ornamental lures, glittering now like medallions of honor.

"Take a good look, Hal," said C.K. softly. "That there is a *Bible* kind of fish."

Harold was in the depths of dejection as they walked back toward the house. "Shoot," he muttered, "ain't nobody ever gonna catch that bullhead."

But the resilient C.K. was in a jaunty mood. He looked at Harold in mild surprise. "Oh yeah, we git 'im now," he said with genuine optimism, "we git 'im for sure . . . now that ah onto his stump-move."

21

III

THE CATTLE AUCTIONEER looked like some-
one who might have been sent from a theatrical casting-
agency — but this was part of his authenticity. Rope-lean,
and deeply tanned, wearing a small white crimped Stetson,
tinted shades, fringed buckskin jacket, drawstring tie, ornamental Spanish-leather boots, with his pant-leg tucked
into one of them to reveal its top-of-the-line Tex-Mex quality, he resembled a combination rancher and carnival pitchman, which was, more or less, the fact of the matter. He
carried a lightweight walking stick, which he used to point
out the characteristics of the animal he was selling, moving
the stick quickly from one hand to the other, with consum-
mate skill and dexterity, as though he were performing a
complex sleight of hand — all part of his charm and spiel,
which was rapid-fire and interspersed with jokes and jibes
of a personal nature concerning the crowd — they who sat
on the top rail of the corral fence, or stood next to it, most
of whom he knew by name.

Assisting the auctioneer, herding the livestock from the
stable into the corral, was an ancient Texas wrangler and

a ten-year-old Mexican boy. The boy would bring in the calf, or steer, by a rope halter, then pass it to the old wrangler, who would lead the animal around the corral for the crowd to see, while the boy went to get another one as the auctioneer began: "Now then, here's a fine little — git 'im settled down there, Roy — a mighty fine piece of baby beef, just shy of Grade-A veal — and have you noticed the price of veal lately? All right then, let's open this one at fifty . . . fifty dollars for this veal on the hoof . . . do I have fifty? Do I have —"

"Thirty dollars."

"I have thirty, who'll say thirty-five?"

"Thirty-two fifty."

"Thirty-two fifty from the Ace-High Ranch — howdy, Ed, good to see you, how's the missus — do I hear thirty-five?"

Inside the livery stable, Harold and C.K. were hanging over the side of a pen that held about twenty head, scrutinizing one six-week-old whiteface calf in particular, until Harold turned to C.K. impatiently.

"Well, god dang it, C.K., ain't you gonna say anything?"

C.K. half closed his eyes, and shifted a segment of straw protruding between his teeth. "Ah waitin' for you to tell me," he said.

Harold stared at him for a minute, frowning in annoyance at having to make the decision himself; then he sighed and looked back at the calf.

"Well, I like 'im . . . leastways better'n that shorthorn you keep yammerin' about. . . . I think he'd make more beef, don't you?"

C.K. remained silently cool, eyes half-closed, blade of grass between his lips; then he pointed to the calf.

"You see where his chest start, and how deep it go?"

"Well, what the heck you think I'm talkin' about?" Harold demanded.

C.K. continued unfazed: "And you see how his hind-quarter set so full?"

"Well, how come you was carryin' on like a mad dog 'bout that shorthorn back yonder?"

" 'Cause when ah carrin' on 'bout that shorthorn . . . ah ain't seen this one yet. You got to take things as they come — you unnerstan' what ah say?"

Outside, leaning against the corral fence, they waited for the calf to be brought in.

"Dang," said Harold, "I done forgot his number!"

"You ain't buyin' a number, boy — you buyin' a calf. Don't worry, ah tell you when he come up."

"Well, what the heck was his number, C.K.?"

"Twenty . . . *seben*," said C.K., very deliberately, with a look of exaggerated weariness.

"Oh yeah, that's right — twenty-seven. Listen, C.K., you think Dad ought to see 'im first?"

"Nope."

"How come?"

" 'Cause he tole *you* to pick him."

"Well, I know that."

"Now, ain't that what he said? He said, 'You pick 'im, Hal.' Ain't that right?"

"Well, I just said so, didn't I? Dang it, C.K., you get crazier all the time!"

"Anyway, here he come now."

"Our calf?"

"Naw, hee-hee — yoah daddy."

They watched Harold's father move along the corral fence, exchanging greetings with acquaintances as he came.

"We found a good 'un, Dad," said Harold, with enthusiasm and what he hoped was a trace of authority.

"You did, huh?" said Harold's father, and he turned to C.K. "Is that right, C.K.?"

"Yessuh, look good to me . . . if they don't bid 'im up too high." He nodded his head toward the stable. "They bringin' him in now."

"Aw-right," said the auctioneer, drawing it out for emphasis, "here we are, number twenty-seven . . . a mighty fine little calf, and prime on the hoof if I ever seen it, courtesy of Big Bill Thompson over at the Aces and Eights, and I can tell you one thing — you can see straight off that this here calf has a mighty lot of *pure Hereford* in him, and that means meat on the table or top dollar in your pocket, and you can't beat either of them propositions today even if your name is H. L. Hunt. Awright, let's kick it off with a fifty-dollar bill — do I have fifty?"

Harold's father leaned over and whispered in his ear: "Bid thirty-five dollars."

Harold cleared his throat. "Thirty-five dollars."

"I have thirty-five," said the auctioneer, "do I hear —"

"Forty," said someone else.

"Forty, I have forty."

Harold looked at his father.

"Go forty-two fifty."

"Forty-two fifty," said a third bidder, before Harold could speak.

"Forty-two fifty, I have forty-two fifty, do I hear forty-five?"

"Well, go on, Son."

"Forty-five."

"Forty-seven fifty."

"Dang," said Harold softly.

"I have forty-seven fifty, do I hear fifty dollars? Do I hear fifty? This is prime-on-the-hoof. We are talking Grade-A, it will bring top dollar, do I hear fifty for this part-Hereford calf?"

Harold's father frowned. "Well, I ain't never paid fifty dollars for a bull-calf in my life," he muttered.

"All in at forty-seven fifty?" said the auctioneer. "Going at forty-seven fifty . . ." He slowly raised his stick.

"Well god damn," said Harold's father, "might as well go whole hog."

Harold gulped. "Fifty," he said, just loud enough.

Harold and C.K. rode in the cab of the Ford pickup, with Harold's father at the wheel. Harold, sitting in the middle, kept turning around to look at his calf tethered in the back of the truck. They drove through the dusk of Texas farmland, corn on one side, cotton on the other.

"Ole Newgate corn sure need rain, don't it," said C.K. squinting at it as they passed. "Some of it look right stunted."

"Well," said Harold's father, "I *told* him he oughtta put a irrigation ditch down through that stretch. Offered to help him do it . . ." He shook his head. "Hell, you can't tell Les Newgate nothin'."

"Do look like we git some rain though," said C.K., sniffing the air, "this east wind hold up a spell longer."

Ahead of them in the distance now, stepping out from the woodlot beyond the cornfield, was a tall man carrying a shotgun. Harold, just turning around, saw him first. "Look," he said, pointing, "ain't that him? Ain't that Les?"

"Well, it looks like 'im, don't it?" said his father.

"Huntin' somethin' outta season, I bet," said Harold.

"Reckon a man can hunt when and what he's a mind to on his own land," said his father.

When Les heard the sound of the pickup, he turned and waited for them.

"You boys git in the back with that fifty-dollar calf," said Harold's father when they reached where Les was waiting.

"Well, dang it, Dad," said Harold, "I reckon I can set up here with you all . . ."

"Git on now," said his father.

In the rear of the pickup, Harold and C.K. sat with their backs against the tailgate, opposite the calf, which was teth-ered to each side of the truck so it wouldn't fall down.

"Shoot," said Harold. "I bet that calf is gonna dress out prime. What'll we call 'im?"

"Well now, Hal, you don't wantta go gittin' too *a*-tached to a animal you gonna wind up eatin' or sellin'."

Harold gave him a look of exasperation. "Heck, you don't think I would, do you?"

C.K. nodded. "Uh-huh, ah do."

"You're crazy," said Harold, and after a minute, he added: "I'm gonna enter 'im in the livestock show at the next Onion. Shoot, I bet he could win a ribbon."

C.K. laughed. "What you gonna do with yoah ole ribbon?"

"Huh?" said Harold in surprise.

"You give it to some little ole gal, ah bet. Hee-hee!"

Harold made a grimace of distaste. "Dang, you really are crazy, C.K."

"You give it to a gal, she jest tie it in her hair an' strut her stuff . . . hee-hee."

"Shoot," said Harold, and looked away.

IV

EXCEPT for Sunday dinner, or at Christmastime and Thanksgiving, the family had all their meals at the round oilcloth-covered table in the kitchen — a modest but comfortable and cheerful room, with a huge wood-burning cook-stove, which was nearly always going. A kerosene lamp was suspended from the ceiling above the table, and two more were in brackets on opposite walls of the room.

At supper that night, Harold's grandfather, a lean and hawklike man of eighty, skin tough and brown as leather, his humor sharp — mischievous and cantankerous by turn — bent forward, eyes glinting from Harold to his father and back, and demanded: "What in the goddam Sam Hill is all this about a fifty-dollar calf?"

Harold's father frowned. "Where'd you hear 'bout that?"

"Ha!" The old man chewed furiously at an ear of corn. "At the barbershop! Not in this house! Nobody around here tells me a goddam thing!"

"Now Granddad," said Harold's mother, "it's not that we don't tell, it's just that your hearin' is beginnin' to fail you."

The old man cupped one hand to his ear in an exaggerated manner. "What say?" he almost shouted.

Harold's mother sighed. "I said —"

He interrupted her by slapping the table triumphantly. "I heard ye! It's a *joke*, you silly goose!" He wiped his mouth on the back of his cuff, excited at having tricked her.

Harold had to laugh; so did his father.

"He can hear awright," said Harold's father, "when he's a mind to — it's just when he don't want to hear that he's suddenly struck post-deaf."

His wife nodded. "I could of told you that much all along."

The old man ignored them both. "Well, I'll tell you one thing," he said. "There ain't a man livin' or dead who ever broke even raisin' a fifty-dollar calf — and that is a natural fack!"

"It ain't for the money, Granddad," Harold explained. "This here is for a Four-H project."

His granddad scoffed. "Four-H! Well, I told you what that 'H' stands for, didn't I? 'Horse's Ass'! Ha!"

"Aw, they been pretty good," said Harold loyally, and turned to his father. "Ain't they, Dad?"

"Don't say 'ain't,' Son," said his mother.

"Yep, they have," said Harold's father, "and that's a fact. Saved us a breech-born heifer a while back. One of their fellers was here to look at our feedlot setup, when that young black-and-white's time come on her right sudden — three days early by the calendar — and I was over to Farney with Les, nobody here but Son and C.K. . . . Hell, they hadn't never worked no breech — we'd of lost the calf for sure, maybe both."

"Aw, we could of done it," muttered Hal. "C.K. seen it done once."

"Well now, Son, that's as may be — but the plain fact is, that Four-H guy stepped in there and did it, and I feel obliged to him."

The old man scoffed. "Wal, I'm glad to hear they're good for somethin'. Last time I talked to one of 'em, he didn't know his ass from a posthole!"

"Granddad," said Harold's mother, "I do wish you wouldn't talk like that — in front of the boy."

"Boy?" exclaimed the old man, grimacing. "Why I bet he can cuss up a blue norther he's a mind to!" He peered at Harold. "Ain't you 'bout thirteen now?"

"Yessir — goin' on."

"He's *twelve*," said his mother firmly, "and he's still a child."

"Why hell, woman, time I was his age I'd been to ever cathouse — 'sportin'-house,' we called 'em then — in this county . . . and a few over the line to boot!"

"Well now that's a big lie, and you know it," said Harold's mother.

"You been yet, boy?" demanded his grandfather.

"Aw, they done closed all them places down," said Harold, without thinking, then glanced at his father. "Leastways I reckon they have."

His mother stood up, looking at him, as she started clearing things away. "Well, now what on earth would you know about that kind of thing anyway?"

Harold was slightly flustered. "No, what I meant was that I heard . . ."

As his voice began to trail away, old Granddad, eyes

bright, ignored her remark and leaned forward, one talon-finger raised on a hand gnarled and dark as wood, and gave Harold a narrow look. "Closed 'em down? Wal, I'll tell you one thing, boy — you travel this wide world over, and wherever you find men, women, and money . . . you're gonna find a whorehouse — and that is a goddam natural fack!"

He looked from one to the other for affirmation. Harold's father was ambivalent; he cleared his throat. "Well, Pa, things have changed a mite since . . . since then."

"Not that," said the old man sharply. "That ain't changed, that can't never change."

"Oh, Grandpa," said Harold's mother, "don't keep talkin' so silly. Anyhow, Harold already has his eye on a girl. Isn't that right, Son?"

"Huh?" said Harold, in complete surprise.

"Why that nice little Sara Jean Johnson," said his mother, "the one you was in the school play with. . . . She sure is a pretty thing."

Moving from the table to the sink, she stopped, turned, looked at the three of them, then past them into the distance, her face taking on the veiled radiance of fond recollection.

"Do you know," she said softly, "I can remember just as plain as day" — looking at Harold now — "the two of you standing there on the stage, when you handed her that bunch of bluebonnets . . . with the white summer dress and her big blue eyes shinin' . . . it was like *she* was a bunch of bluebonnets too . . ."

Harold and his father regarded her curiously, while Grandfather resumed eating with gusto. And then his mother came out of her reverie to ask: "But you do like her, don't you, Son?"

"Why I ain't even seen —" He corrected himself. "I *habn't* even seen her since that play."

"Well," said his mother with cheerful reassurance, "you'll probably see her at one of the church socials. You have another look — she's a mighty pretty little thing."

She turned back to the sink, and Grandfather leaned toward Harold. "Hell, I'll find out if they've shut 'em down — an' then I'll tell you where they moved 'em to!"

"Now, Pa," said Harold's father, "don't go puttin' him up to that — cost enough awready just keepin' him in *clothes*, growin' like a beanstalk." He looked at Harold, as this thought took him to another concern. "Them huntin' boots gonna take you through next winter, Son? Your toes touchin' the end yet?"

Harold was embarrassed at all the attention. "Aw, I think they'll be okay."

"Well, I gotta pair of insulateds," his father went on, "that's just a might snug on me . . . probably fit you about right."

Harold's mother came back over, continuing to clear away the table.

"Why now those would be way too big for Harold," she said. "Besides he don't want old hand-me-down boots. Do you, Son?"

"Hand-me-down hell," said his father irately. "Them's *L. L. Bean's.* Cost me thirty-seven fifty . . . Why, they got five good years' wear left in 'em. At the very least."

Grandfather slapped the table. "L. L. Bean! Now there's a first-rate outfit if there ever was one! I had a pair of their insulateds lasted me twelve goddam years, hard wear, an' that's a fack!"

"Well, even so," said Harold's mother, "everybody likes to have their own things . . ."

"Well, damn it all," said Grandfather suddenly to Harold, "what I want to know is more about that fifty-dollar calf! What's he got — two tallywhackers? Ha!"

"No," said Harold, "but I think he's got a whole lot of *pure Hereford* in 'im. . . . Don't you, Dad?"

"Yep, mighty fine-lookin' calf."

"An' I'll tell you somethin' else," said the old man. "Half-breed stock'll never dress out prime. Not unless it's grain-fed, an' there ain't nobody fool enough to do that, at today's price of corn."

"Well, I'm gonna raise 'im good," said Harold, "an' enter 'im in the stock show next year . . ." He smiled shyly. "Maybe win us a ribbon, who knows?"

"*Ribbon!*" said Granddad, scoffing and snorting. "Well now you just try choppin' up some of them ribbons, hang 'em in the smokehouse, an' see how far through the winter they git you!"

V

LATE afternoon, C.K. and Harold slowly walked a two-mile length of fence, looking for a break in the barbed wire, where the stock were sometimes getting out. Harold was bored and listless. "Heck, I can't see where they're breakin' through."

But C.K. was unperturbed. "Oh ah reckon we come 'cross it sooner or later," he said. "We just sneak up on it."

They reached a section of the fence where it bent slightly, then stretched away, unbroken, as far as the eye could see. Harold sighted along each strand, then straightened up with a disgruntled sigh. "Well, it sure as heck ain't down that stretch."

C.K. leaned over to confirm it. "Naw," he agreed, "be no use in walkin' that stretch." He stared out across the adjacent field. "Reckon we jest as well cut on over . . . thata ways."

Harold looked at him briefly. "I reckon you mean over toward the tank?"

C.K. frowned and shrugged, not looking at the boy.

"Well shoot, if we cain't find no break, we cain't find no break — now ain't that right?"

"Is that all you ever think about?" asked Harold, trying to sound more responsible. "Catchin' that old bullhead catfish?"

C.K. regarded him with mock surprise. "What? You done give up on that bullhead? Shoot, Hal, I sho' thought you had more gumption than that."

They climbed over the fence, and set off into the pasture that bordered the pond. They walked in silence, until Harold stopped to squint into the distance, where a number of cows were grazing; there was one cow, however, apart from the others, lying on its stomach, with its head stretched out on the ground in front of it.

"What's wrong with that dang cow?" Harold demanded.

C.K. shaded his eyes with his hand and took a long look.

"She do seem to be takin' it easy, don't she?"

They changed direction slightly and began walking toward her. "Look like ole Maybelle," C.K. said, squinting his eyes at the distance.

"Well, I ain't never seen a cow act like that before," said Harold, mystified. ". . . layin' there with her head on the ground like a damned old hound-dog."

The cow didn't move when they reached it, just stared up at them; she was chewing her cud, in a rhythmic and contented manner.

"Look at that dang cow," Harold muttered, ever impatient with enigma, ". . . it is old Maybelle, ain't it?" He felt her nose and then began kicking her gently on the flank. "Git up, dang it."

"Sho' is," said C.K., leaning over and patting her neck. "What's the matter with you, Maybelle?"

Then C.K. saw it, a bush of it, about twenty feet away, growing in the midst of a patch of dwarf cactus, and he went over and began to examine it with great care.

"This here is a full-growed plant," he said, touching it in several places, gently bending it back, almost caressingly. Finally he stood up, hands on his hips, looking back at the prostrate cow.

"Must be mighty fine gage," he said.

"Well, I ain't never seen no locoweed make a cow act like that," said Harold, as if his own inexperience in the matter could somehow nullify what had happened to Maybelle, and he began absently kicking at the plant.

"That ain't no ordinary locoweed," said C.K., ". . . that there is *red-dirt marijuana*, that's what that is."

Harold spat, frowning. "Shoot," he said, "I reckon we oughtta pull it up and burn it."

"I reckon we oughtta," said C.K. with a sigh.

They pulled it up.

"Don't gen'lly take to red-dirt," C.K. remarked casually, brushing his hands. "They say if it do, then it's mighty fine indeed — they reckon it's got to be strong to do it, you see."

"Must be pretty dang *strong* awright," Harold dryly agreed, looking back at the disabled cow. "You think we oughtta git Doc Parks?"

They walked over to the cow.

"Shoot," said C.K., "they ain't nothin' wrong with *this* cow."

The cow had raised her head, and her eyes followed them when they were near. They stared down at her for a minute or two, and she looked at them, interestedly, still chewing.

"Ole Maybelle havin' a *fine* time," said C.K., leaning over to stroke her muzzle. "Hee-hee. She *high*, that's what she is." He straightened up again. "Ah tell you right now, boy, you lookin' at a ver' contented cow there."

"You reckon it's ruin her milk?" Harold wanted to know.

"Shoot, that red-dirt gage make her milk all the more rich. Yeah, she goin' give some Grade-A milk indeed after that kinda relaxation. Ain't that right, Maybelle?"

They started toward the fence, Harold dragging the bush of locoweed along beside him, swinging it back and forth, while C.K. looked at it in bemusement — spiced perhaps with genuine interest.

"Jest look at the ole root on that plant!" he said, laughing. "Big ole juicy root — sho' would make a fine soup-bone! Hee-hee!"

He had twisted off a branch of the plant and plucked a little bunch of leaves from it, which he was chewing now, like mint.

"What's it taste like?" asked Harold.

C.K. plucked another small bunch and proffered it to the boy.

"Here you is, my man," he said.

"Naw, it jest makes me sick," said Harold, thrusting his free hand into his pocket and making a face; so, after a minute, C.K. put that piece in his mouth too.

"We could dry it out an *smoke* it," said Harold.

C.K. laughed. "Yes," he said flatly, "ah reckon we could."

"Let's dry it out and sell it," the boy went on.

C.K. looked at him, plaintive exasperation dark in his face.

"Now Hal, don't go talkin' without you knows what you talkin' about."

"We could sell it to them Mex'can sharecroppers over at Farney," said Harold. "They all smoke it."

"Hal, what is you talkin' about — them people ain't got no money."

They went over the fence again, silent for a while.

"Well, don't you wantta dry it out?" Harold asked, child of twelve, yearning for action, projects, planning . . .

C.K. shook his head. "Boy, you don't catch me givin' no advice on that kinda business — you daddy run me right off this place somethin' like that ever happen."

Harold started breaking it up.

"We'd have to put it someplace," he said, "where the dang stock wudn't git at it."

C.K. nodded sagely. "Don't want *nobody* foolin' with it."

Harold sighed. "We don't want nobody to *find* it."

"That's jest what ah say," said C.K.

"No, you didn't." Harold wished to correct him. "There's a difference between somebody *findin'* it an somebody *foolin'* with it. Don't you know that?"

"They is a difference," C.K. agreed. "If they don't find it, they don't fool with it."

Not entirely satisfied, Harold was ready to pursue it, but C.K. stayed him with a raised hand. "An' ah know jest where we put it." He gestured toward a huge sycamore tree directly ahead. "Up in the ole tree-house tree. Ain't nobody gonna go up in there. Right, Hal?"

Harold seemed to consider it for a moment before he spoke. "That's fer sure," he said.

Now they were beneath the great tree, looking up to where its high canopy spread above them like a giant's umbrella, the outermost branches swaying slowly in an imperceptible wind. So, after C.K. secured the root of the big plant under his belt, cinching it carefully as if for a walk on the moon, they started up, climbing what was left of a crude ladder of short narrow boards nailed to the trunk of the tree.

"Ah wudn't go puttin' a whole lotta faith in these here ladder-steps," C.K. cautioned, after he had yanked one of them off the tree and tossed it to the ground. But they continued without incident until they were almost halfway up, already high enough to see the distant tree-circled pond and, in another direction, Les Newgate's barn, and Harold paused, his hand resting tentatively on the next makeshift rung of these ladder-steps, thinking that if it was at all loose he would jerk it out and fling it with a powerful motion to the side that would cause it to sail from the tree like the deadly boomerang of some ancient hunting tribe — thinking this, and in his mind's eye, seeing it, the movement of his arm, and the whistling trajectory of the weapon, when he became aware of a startling reality: about three feet away from him, so close he could have leaned out and touched it — or much, much worse, could have accidentally hit it with his pretend boomerang — was the largest hornets' nest he had ever seen, so big indeed that it was at first unrecognizable as such, a deathly gray cocoon of monstrous proportions — the shape of a football but somewhat larger. It was, in fact, so uncommonly large that C.K., two rungs above, had passed without noticing it. But he saw it now.

"That there," he said quietly, "belong in a sideshow."

Seen in this perspective, so alarmingly close, the hornets' nest appeared unreal — as if conceived and constructed by a bizarre master-artist, using only papier-mâché:

either layer after layer molded into a solid mass, or stretched as a gray membrane over some painstaking skeletal armature; impossible to tell which, because the whole thing had no apparent use or function, like a monolith designed merely to celebrate pure and unadorned symmetry. It would not be until one perceived that at the very base of this structure of seamless perfection was a black hole the size of a silver dollar — not until then that one might suspect something less theoretical, something strangely exotic was at hand; but still without menace — that is, until the arrival of a single hornet, ribbed with black and gold, large enough, at close range, to be considered as an individual being, with weight, texture, eyes, mandibles, antennas, and, all too apparent in its quavering anticipation, a thornlike stinger at the tail. And when the hornet crawls, slowly, and seemingly with great confidence, down the surface of the nest and into the black hole, it is only then that one becomes inescapably aware of the true nature of this edifice, and its potential for apocalyptic horror. For someone like Harold or C.K. — no strangers to the trauma of a hornet encounter — the sight and proximity of the great nest was as momentous as it was ineffable. Only C.K. could have been irrepressible enough to say, "We come back tonight an' put a stopper in that hole, then drop it down ole Les Newgate chimney! Hee-hee-hee." The image, as farfetched as it was, made Harold shudder slightly as he eased himself up the next rung.

Near the top they reached a wide three-limbed crook in the big tree. Large rusting nails protruded from two of the limbs — the last remnants of an ill-fated tree-house of yesteryear.

"We use these ole tree-house spikes hook the plant onto," said C.K., and he began to do so.

41

"Ah bet you done forgit the ole tree-house, Hal," he added, knowing it wasn't entirely true.

"Oh sure," said Harold, "I jest wish I *could* forgit the dang thing." His mind flooded with fragments of unwanted recollection even as he spoke.

But C.K. deprecated the notion with a wave of his hand. "All them things was jest part of growin' up 'round here, Hal," he assured him. But Harold was by no means convinced of that. The tree-house had been built — for his eighth birthday — by his father and C.K., working late into the long summer evenings when it stayed light right up to almost nine o'clock, using the old boards from a derelict chickenhouse and limbs cut from the tree itself. But his real present that year was his first gun, a single-shot .22 rifle — each of these things being a widely practiced Texas tradition; namely, that a boy be given his first gun at eight, and that it be a single-shot .22 rifle. This was considered both manly and prudent — manly in that it was an actual gun, not an air rifle, and prudent in that it was a gun of the smallest caliber, and like his hand-me-down twenty-gauge, a single shot.

For the first six months or so, he was not allowed to shoot the .22 unless he was with C.K. or his father. If he wanted to go out shooting on his own, he had to use his BB gun — a Daisy air rifle, manufactured to resemble a pump-action shotgun, that shot copper-coated pellets a scant forty yards or so, but with at least bird-killing power. Except for the farm animals, he was allowed to shoot almost anything that moved. He was discouraged from shooting certain birds: hummingbirds, mockingbirds, and whippoorwills; all others he was more or less encouraged to shoot because presumably he was training his eye for the time when he would be good enough to shoot dove with a .22. Dove, like quail, was a great dinner-table favorite, and a good shot with a .22 would pick them off a tree branch, one at a time, and in some cases could take the heads clean off — "and without," in his grandfather's words, "ruffling a single feather."

The first winter after the tree-house was built was one of the coldest in Texas history — "the year of the Big Blue Norther," it was called. Milk froze in the pail between the barn and the house. On the third morning of the norther, Harold went out to collect the eggs from the chickenhouse; he opened the door and was astonished to find the white leghorns sitting on the ten-foot perch in perfect alignment, like cutouts at a shooting gallery, frozen solid. C.K. came into the chickenhouse while he was still standing there perplexed.

Harold gave him a look of concern. "We gotta thaw 'em out," he said.

"Cain't be done," said C.K. "Them birds be long gone."

"We could thaw 'em out in the oven," Harold went on unconvinced; but C.K. was adamant.

"Nope," he said, "ah seen this happen onct before durin' a real cold spell . . ." He crossed to the perch. "But ah gonna show you sumpthin' ver' funny, Hal, hee-hee. Now jest watch this . . ."

He reached out to the perch and gently pushed the near-est bird backward, then the second one — and each in turn executed a full 360-degree vertical spin, revolving on claws that were locked frozen around the perch in a perfect ring.

"Are you crazy?" Harold had demanded, but he was soon trying it himself.

And now that image, of hens doing frozen loop-the-loops, caused a torrent of memory — all connected to his grandfather's ranting rampage against the deer that had ravaged the apple orchard.

"Boy, I want you to rent me out a corner of that tree-house of yours," he had said.

Harold had a notion of what he wanted to do, because he had heard his father say to Les Newgate even before the structure was finished: "I'll tell you one thing — usin' that open field straight ahead down there, this would make one hell of a deer-stand. A four-power scope an' you could knock their ears off!"

And Les Newgate had looked it over and said: "Well, I reck-*tum*."

"Now this deal is gonna be just between you an' me," his grandfather had explained. "You don't need to say anything about it to your mother."

Harold was surprised at the precaution.

"How come?" he wanted to know.

His grandfather, who often had a chaw of Red Man in his mouth, had given a long slow spit.

"Your mother," he said quietly, "is a mighty fine woman, I reckon you know that?"

"Yes sir."

"But there is one thing that she does not, to this very day, unnerstan' *whatsoever!*"

He paused, adjusting the chaw, pausing long enough so that Harold was obliged to look at him expectantly and even to ask, "What's that?"

"That a *deer*," the old man went on carefully, "is a *varmint*."

"A varmint? You mean like a woodchuck or a possum?" His grandfather had nodded vigorously. "That's right!" he said in the kind of barking tone he sometimes used for emphasis. "That's right! They *will rob you blind!*"

As soon as the norther had let up, it had begun to snow — an icy mist of a snow, but enough to turn everything a shimmering white.

"Now be when he git the first deer," C.K. said, "after he put out his *setup*."

Between the tree-house and the pond was a stretch of unfenced field too rocky for pasture. A woodlot bordered the field, and it was there, on the edge of the woodlot, just into the field, that the old man put out his "setup" — which consisted of a bale of hay, a scattering of rotten apples, and, "just to be on the safe side," he had said with a chuckle, a twenty-five-pound salt lick. Then he leveled his flat-shooting 243 Winchester, with his special hand-load, out the tree-house window, clamped it down, and zeroed in on the setup — firing at a dead branch he had stuck in the ground so that the end of it was about two feet above, and two feet to the side of, the salt lick. When he had adjusted and readjusted the windage and elevation so that he clipped the top of the branch three times in a row, he screwed the clamp down tight.

"That way he go for the heart-shot," C.K. had explained. "He done study it out."

"Well, how come you know so all-fired much about it?" Harold asked.

C.K. tilted his head back and half closed his eyes.
" 'Cause you see ah work on the setup a'fore now. You daddy use the setup onct a few years back. Ah hep with it. You wudn't two, three year ole at the time. You gonna

see some good shootin', Hal, if he let us stay up here with him. They say you gran'daddy don't miss."

But Harold was not overly impressed.

"It don't look all that faraway to me," he said concerning the distance to the setup. "I bet it ain't any farther than that hunnert-yard bull's-eye target we used with the twenty-two."

"Well, that's as may be," said C.K. with genial authority, "but your gran'daddy be goin' for a *pre*-cise shot, you see — either to the heart or right behin' the ear. He got to git 'im with jest one shot, you see."

In exchange for their assistance — carrying out the bale of hay, the salt lick, and the bag of apples — and for their promise to help drag away the carcasses, his grandfather had let Harold and C.K. sit with him in the tree-house; in fact, he had encouraged them, to the great irritation of Harold's mother, to spend the previous night, in order that the place would not be "colder than a witch's tit" when he got there in the morning at slightly before dawn. And they had made a big thing of it, Harold and C.K., bringing pallets and blankets, and a Coleman lantern for warmth, camping out, with C.K. even wearing on his belt an old army canteen that Harold's grandfather gave him for the occasion. So that what had begun as a mere notion — sitting with the old man during his vigil — had become something of an adventure: a winter night in a tree-house — quite an unheard of occurrence in these parts, but, as it turned out, most enjoyable; the Coleman lantern gave off a soft golden-orange glow of warmth. Outside, the night wind might whistle eerily in the branches of the tree all around them, and carry from afar the crazed threats of screech owl and coyote, but inside the golden glow of the tree-house, snug in their blankets, Harold and C.K. were feeling no pain.

"Mighty cozy heah," said C.K.

"Yep," Harold agreed, but added a minute later: "That dang screech owl is sure close, ain't he?"

"Now, Hal, don't start up," said C.K. "Them is jest night sounds. Screech owl be lookin' for his supper. He lookin' for squirrel an' mouse . . . an' for little snake . . ." He laughed softly. "And coyote lookin' for him."

Although the tree-house had been carefully and sturdily built, its construction was such that there were enough cracks between the boards to afford a good view of whatever might happen in the distant field. And after Harold's grandfather had arrived and sat down behind his Winchester, they did not have long to wait. The layer of fine white mist that shrouded that part of the field where the enticements had been placed had gradually drifted away as the morning light grew stronger; and what was revealed at once, as though it had been standing there all along, standing on a stage, waiting for the curtain to rise, was a magnificent male deer — a large buck that stood with raised head, its nostrils flared and releasing small puffs of steamed breath into the cold morning air — nostrils that appeared to have a fix on the pungent aroma of the putrefying apples, or perhaps the sweet crisp delicacy of the baled alfalfa. Harold watched as the deer started to move forward, slow and tentative, like an undecided dancer, very careful, as if aware of a certain vulnerability. Inside the tree-house the click was audible when his grandfather moved the safety on the gun, and the shot, two seconds later, was deafening. The deer collapsed, its legs simply folding beneath it.

"Mighty fine shot, Mistuh Steven," C.K. was the first to say.

"It sure was, Granddad," said Harold, unsure what to say, this being his first experience in such a matter.

By the time they reached the deer, it was lying on its side, its legs now straight out. Harold had been the first down the tree and he was the first to reach the deer. While still some distance away, he had made out the rising steam, created, as he knew, by breath from the deer's mouth and nostrils — but when he got much closer he saw that it was also coming from somewhere else. The deer was lying on its right side, so that the side its heart was on was up, toward the sky, and there, on the deer's chest, just behind the upper foreleg, was the hole made by the bullet; and blood was pumping out of the hole — rising an inch or so in small regular spasms, each creating a puff of steam when it hit the cold air.

Harold stayed a few feet away, resting on one knee, waiting for the others to arrive, which they did almost immediately. C.K. dropped down beside him and his grandfather paused there as well, breathing hard after his brisk walk from the tree-house.

"Ain't a bad-lookin' buck, is he?" he said. "Eight-pointer, I reckon . . ." And he crossed over to it, knelt down, leaned forward, and put his mouth over the blood-flowing wound. "You don't git too many like this," he said, wiping his mouth with the back of his hand. "You gotta take advantage." He gave them a sly grin. "C.K., you wantta bring your canteen cup over here."

"Yes suh," said C.K., removing it from his belt as he took it over.

The blood, which still rose out of the wound in rhythmic surges, had slowed noticeably, but the old man was able to half fill the canteen cup before it stopped. He handed the cup to Harold.

"Old Indian custom," he said. "Ain't no taste like it."

Harold put the cup to his lips and tilted it. He had already decided he did not want to swallow it no matter how it tasted. Truth to tell, he did not even want to taste it, but he could see there was no getting out of that. He tried to hold the liquid against his upper lip, letting only the smallest sip into his mouth, hoping it would look like a respectable swallow. The taste was warm, sick-sweet, and salty at the same time. Instead of swallowing it, he tried to just keep it somewhere in his mouth, under his tongue and around his gums. And he passed the cup to C.K.

While C.K. was still dealing with it, Harold's father and Les Newgate had come up, each wanting a sip; Harold's father had one, and passed it to Les.

"Is she still hot, Les?" the old man asked.

"Yep," said Les, finishing it off in a gulp and wiping his mouth. "No taste like it. That boy git any?"

"Sure as hell did," said the old man, sounding proud of it. "An' C.K. too."

Harold's father laughed. "Well, C.K.," he said. "You may be the only nigger in this county to ever taste hot deer blood."

C.K. laughed aloud at the notion. "I reckon you may be right about that," he said.

"I'll bet he's the best one too," said Harold, uncomfortable that his father had used the word.

"Boy, I know that," said his father in a flash of irritation. "Why hell, C.K. is family."

Next to him Les Newgate was still licking his lips. "Well, I'll tell you one thing," he drawled, looking at Harold with a crazy grin. "They say a man can git *right drunk* on hot deer blood!"

That use of the tree-house as a sort of backyard deer-stand marked the beginning of its decline. Harold's mother, ordinarily a woman of placid temperament, was upset.

"What if Aunt Flora had been here?" she had demanded, referring to her sister from Dallas who sometimes came for a visit. "And little Caddy? What would they have thought about luring deer up like that, with a salt lick and so on, and then killing them?" When she inadvertently heard about the hot-deer-blood incident, she just said, "Good Lord!" and did not want to hear any more about it.

So after getting a second deer, and filling their locker with venison, Harold's grandfather took the salt lick back to the barn. The hay and the apples soon disappeared, bringing to a close the days of the setup. Harold overheard his grandfather explaining it to Les Newgate: "The boy's mother was havin' a tizzy-fit about twice a day. I finally threw in the goddam towel."

"Reckon she'll change her mind," said Les, "when they's no more apple fer her pies."

"That's right, that's right!" the old man barked and slapped his leg.

But even in the absence of inducements, deer would occasionally cross the field, presenting those rare targets of opportunity, so much more dramatic and tempting than the ones at the County Fair shooting gallery, and indeed Harold did finally succumb — shooting his birthday .22 rifle out of the tree-house window and making a good shot, but on what proved to be a pregnant doe — resulting in much hullabaloo and chastisement.

Not long after that misfortune, Harold and Big Lawrence, his friend from in town, had been horsing around inside the tree-house, wrestling and shoving and pummeling each other, not in anger but with great enthusiasm, and Harold had fallen, out the door and all the way to the ground. One of the lower limbs of the tree fortunately broke his fall, but also his left arm. At that point it had been decided that, all things considered, the tree-house might be a bad influence on a growing boy, and it was dismantled.

Now, almost five years later, the events were like a hazy afterglow to Harold as he and C.K. walked back toward the house, the big marijuana plant stashed in the sycamore behind them.

"Listen, Hal," said C.K. about halfway on, "ah tell you right now, you don't wanna say nothin' 'bout this to nobody up to the house. Or to Big Lawrence or any you other frien' in town."

"You mean 'cause it's against the law?"

"That's right," said C.K.

As they walked on, Harold tried to read C.K.'s face for something beyond his answer, but could see nothing. They walked in silence.

"Listen," Harold finally said, "is your brother still in jail?"

C.K. didn't answer at once, just looked at Harold without expression, then nodded. "Uh-huh."

"How come?"

"How come what?"

"How come he's in the dang jail!"

"He ain't in the jail — he in the road gang."

"That's the same thing, ain't it?"

"Worse."

"Well, how come he's there? What'd he do?"

"Nothin'."

"Bull," said Harold, kicking at a rock. "I heard he *killed* somebody . . . for messin' around with Cora Lee Lawson."

C.K. gave him a dull look. "Well then, you know so much about it, why you ask me?"

" 'Cause I just *heard* it — I never said I knowed it for sure." He waited. "How long is he in there for?"

"Oh, he in there for a *long* time," said C.K. He chuckled. "They may of throwed away the key on ole Big Nail."

"Well, how come he's there in the first place?" Harold demanded.

C.K. sighed. "Well, he there mainly 'cause of bad luck, that's how come he there."

The boy scoffed. " 'Bad luck' — you call killin' somebody 'bad luck'?"

"No, the bad luck was when the sheriff come along — jest after it happen. Ain't nobody call the sheriff, he jest come along . . . by bad luck." He looked at Harold to see if he understood, then added: "It weren't no white folks' business, you see, them fightin' like that. The sheriff got no business comin' in there. He jest passin' by in his car, then he see somethin' goin' on, an' come in — but he got no business there."

"Shoot," said Harold, "he's the dang *sheriff*, ain't he? I reckon he can make it his business to go wherever he wants to."

C.K. shook his head firmly. "Nope. Not in there he cain't — not in the Paradise Bar."

Harold had heard this sort of crazy talk before, about how the Paradise Bar was somehow outside the law, or should be.

"You're lucky they don't shut that place down," he said.

C.K. laughed. "Well, they try to shut down the Paradise Bar might cause a lotta trouble. Maybe more than they be ready to handle. Anyhow, why would they want to do that?"

"Why?" Harold seemed surprised. "Because of all the fightin' an' killin' that goes on in there, that's why."

C.K. gave him a sad, quizzical look. "You been in the Paradise Bar, Hal — you ain't never seen no fightin' or killin' in there, has you?"

"No," Harold had to admit, though he was quick to add with firm conviction, "but I've heard plenty."

C.K. nodded. "Uh-huh. Well now they is a big differ-ence, you see, between what a man hear an' what be true. The sooner you learn that, the smarter you be."

They walked on, not speaking, until they reached the last stretch of fence between them and the house. C.K. put his foot on the bottom strand of barbed wire, while lifting the one above it with his hand. "There you is, my man," he said lightly, standing to the side.

Harold stepped through, then held it from the other side for C.K. "What'll we do with that stuff when it's dried out, C.K.?"

C.K. shrugged, kicked at a rock, then thrust his hands into his pockets.

"Shoot," he said, sounding a little like Harold, "ah reckon we find some kinda use for it." And he smiled, quite openly, at the challenging prospect.

VI

HAROLD SAT out on the back steps, in the full blazing heat of the Texas summer, knees up, and propping in between them his old single-load twenty-gauge shotgun. While he steadied and squeezed the butt in one hand, the other, with careful unbroken slowness, wrapped a long piece of friction tape around and around the stock — for beginning at the toe of the butt and stretching up about five inches was a thin dry crack in the old wood.

His mother came out, down off the back porch, carrying a blue-gray chipped enameled basin heaped with twists of wet half-wrung clothes.

"You be careful with that old gun," she said, with a slight frown. "Your daddy know you got it out?"

"He *told* me to get it out," Harold said, his nasal twang making him sound querulous. "Heck, I wanted to use his twelve-gauge double."

"Stop saying 'heck' and 'dang' so much," she replied softly, almost absently, it being perhaps the ten-thousandth time she'd said it. "Twelve years old is too young to use a twelve-gauge shotgun."

"Aw I shoot it all the time, you know that."

"Not unless you're with a grown-up, you don't."

"Well, that ain't exactly my fault, is it?"

"Don't say 'ain't' — you and Lawrence goin' huntin'?"

"Aw just fool around, I guess."

"Where at?"

"I dunno . . . out around Hampton, I reckon."

"You wantta be careful out there, with the planes comin' in and all."

He looked at her in surprise. "They done closed that part of it down, didn't you know that?"

"There's private planes still come in there . . ."

"If there is, I never seen 'em."

"Well, you wantta be careful anyway with that Lawrence — is he still crazy as ever?"

"Aw he's awright."

"How you going to get into town?"

"Gonna ride in with Les Newgate."

"Les goin' in?" his mother asked, through the clothespins in her mouth, not thinking.

"Naw," said Harold, "that's how come I'm gettin' a ride with him . . . cause he ain't goin' in! Ha-ha-ha!"

"Now don't be smart," she said without effort, then started back inside, "and you shouldn't be sittin' here bareheaded in the hot sun, you'll get a stroke."

Big Lawrence lived in the nearest town — Alvarado, population seven hundred and dwindling — six miles away. Just outside town, Les Newgate slowed the pickup and pulled over, so that he and Harold could see how they were setting up tents and booths for the Big Red Onion. This was the county's grandest annual event. Officially, it was named the Johnson County Old Settlers' Reunion, but the children, being unable or unwilling to pronounce it, had begun, as far back as living memory, to call it the Big Red Onion, and the grown-ups had eventually gone along.

"Wal," said Les, "looks like they settin' up the Onion," and he spat a long stream of Red Man chaw from the bulge in his cheek.

"Yep," said Harold.

"I reckon we'll go," said Les, "take the kids over anyhow. Leastways little Billy Bob — he's still young enough to enjoy it. Your granddaddy gonna fiddle this year?"

The Onion featured a livestock-and-produce exhibition, a carnival of rides and games of chance, a midway of concessions featuring oddities of nature — animal and human — dancing girls, and a small-scale rodeo. But the crowning event, for adults anyway, was the Old Fiddlers' Contest, which drew competitors from all over the Southwest — a contest which Harold's grandfather always entered and frequently won.

"I don't rightly know," said Harold. "They ask him if he wanted to be in it, or be a judge. Reckon it's 'cause his 'thritis is actin' up — that's what Momma says."

"I won a five-dollar bet on him last year," said Les.

"I know you did," said Harold.

Les shifted into low, and they started pulling away. "Hard for a man to do his best," he said, "when his hand stiffens up."

"I reckon."

"An' I'll tell you somethin' else too," said Les with genial authority. "Your granddad ain't one who likes to come in no second or third place."

"I know it," said Harold, looking straight ahead.

Harold reached Big Lawrence's house by way of his neighbor's backyard. Stepping through an open place in the fence two houses before, and cutting across, he could hear Lawrence on at the house and he saw his shadow, dark there behind the window screen.

"Ka-*pow!* Ka-*pow!* Ka-*pow!*" was what he heard Big Lawrence say.

An ordinary bedroom, Texas schoolboy motif — guns, sports trophies, boxing gloves, animal skins (all small except for the deer) nailed to the wall, and photographs of ballplayers. Sitting on the bed was Big Lawrence — a rawboned fullback type — and all down around his feet the scattered white patches lay, fallen each like a poisoned cactus-bloom, every other center oil-dark, he cleaning his rifle: .243 Savage.

Across one end of the bed, flat on his stomach, looking at an old comic book, was Crazy Ralph Wilton, while Tommy Sellers sat on the floor, back flat to the wall. Tommy Sellers was an all-county shortstop; he had baseball and glove in his lap, and every so often he would flip the baseball up and twirl it over his fingers like an electric top.

As Harold came in and sat down, on the arm of a stuffed misshapen mohair chair, Lawrence looked up, laughing. Most of the time Lawrence's laugh was coarse and, in a curious way, bitter.

"Well, goddam if it ain't old Harold!" he said, affecting

an even more pronounced Texas drawl than he actually had, perhaps because of a western movie they had seen together a few nights before.

Somewhere, next door, a radio was playing loudly — Saturday-morning cowboy music from station WRR in downtown Big D Dallas.

Crazy Ralph looked from Harold to Lawrence, and back. "You gonna do it again today?" he asked, grinning with a kind of demented slyness.

Lawrence glared at him. "You jest shut your dang hole 'bout that, Ralph."

"*Are* you, Harold?" he repeated, still wild-eyed and grinning. "Y'all gonna do it?"

On the floor, next to the wall, the baseball spun twisting across Tommy Sellers's knuckles like a trained rat.

"I told you to shut your A-fuckin' hole," said Lawrence grimly, slamming the bolt home and slapping it hard. Then he looked at Harold. "Let's head out."

Harold started to get up, but before he could, Lawrence turned around on the bed and leaned heavily against Ralph's legs, sighting the rifle out over the backyard. There, across the yard, sitting about three feet out from the back fence, all crouched with feet drawn under, was a cat — a black cat, rounded, large, and unblinking in the high morning sun. Big Lawrence squeezed one out on the empty chamber. "Ka-pow!" he said, and brought the gun down, laughing. "Goddam! Right in the eye!" He raised up, and taking some shells from his shirt pocket, loaded the rifle; then he quickly threw out the shells, working the action in a jerky, eccentric manner, causing the shells to fly all over the bed. One of them went above the comic book in Ralph's hand and hit the bridge of his nose. The other boys laughed, but Crazy Ralph muttered something, rubbing his nose, and flipped the shell back over into the rest of them next to Lawrence's leg, as he might have done playing marbles — and Big Lawrence flinched.

"You crazy bastard!" said Lawrence, and then he reached over, picked up the shell and threw it as hard as he could against the wall behind Ralph Wilton's head, making him duck. They left the shell where it fell on the floor behind the bed. Ralph didn't speak, just kept turning the pages of the comic book, while Lawrence sat there staring hard at the book in front of Ralph's eyes.

Then Lawrence reloaded the gun and drew another bead out the window. The black cat was still sitting there, head on toward the muzzle, when Lawrence moved the safety with his thumb. Next door someone turned the radio up a little more, but here in the small room, the explosion was loud. The comic book jumped in Crazy Ralph's hand like it had been jerked by a wire. "God*dam* it!" he said, but he didn't look around, just shifted a little, as if settling to the book again.

Harold rested his elbow on the windowsill and looked out across the yard. The cat hardly seemed to have moved — only to have been pushed back hard toward the fence, head down, feet drawn under, eyes staring straight at the house as though hypnotized.

And in the screen now, next to a hole made in opening the screen from the outside, was another, perfectly round, flanged out instead of in, worn suddenly, by the passing of the bullet, all bright silver at the edge.

*   *   *

Big Lawrence and Harold walked a dirt road along one side of the old abandoned Hampton Airport. It was an unbelievably hot, dry day.

"What's a box of shells like that cost?" Lawrence asked, and when Harold told him, Lawrence said: "Sure, but for how many shells?"

At crossroads, the corner of a field, a place where on some Sundays certain people who made model airplanes came to try them, they found, all taped together, five or six shiny old dry-cell batteries as might be used for starting just such small engines.

Harold pulled these batteries apart while they walked on, slower now beneath the terrible sun, and when Lawrence wanted to see if he could hit one of them in the air with the shotgun, they agreed to trade off, three rifle cartridges for one shotgun shell.

Harold pitched one of the batteries up, but Lawrence wasn't ready. "Wait'll I say 'Pull,' " he told Harold.

He stood to one side then, holding the shotgun across his chest as he might have seen done on a TV program about skeet shooting.

"Okay, now . . . Pull!"

Lawrence missed the first one, said that Harold was throwing too hard.

Harold tossed another, gently, lobbing it into the sun, glinting end over gleaming end, a small meteor in slow motion, suddenly jumping with the explosion, this same silver thing, as caught up in a hot air jet, but with the explosion, coughing out its black insides.

"Dead bird," said Big Lawrence.

Harold laughed. "I reckon it is," he said softly.

*　　　*　　　*

Once across the field, away from the airport, they turned up the railroad track. And now they walked very slowly, straight into the firelike sun, mirrored a high blinding silver in the rails that lay for five miles unbending, flat against the shapeless waste, ascending, stretching ablaze to the sun itself — so that seen from afar, as quite small, they could have appeared as innocent children, to walk eternally between two columns of dancing light.

At one place, Lawrence stopped, laid his rifle alongside the tracks, knelt, and pressed his ear against one of the rails. Harold watched him, and Big Lawrence grinned shrewdly up from the rail. "You wantta try it here?" he said.

Harold frowned down at the tracks. "How could we?"

"There's a way," said Lawrence, grinning and nodding.

Harold kicked uncertainly at the rocks between the wooden ties. "Shoot . . . ," he muttered.

"You scared to try it here?" Lawrence asked, sly and secret.

"There's not enough room," said Harold. "It wouldn't go over us."

Lawrence got to his feet, brushed his hands, and picked up the rifle. "Okay, we'll do it down at the trestle," he said, and they walked on.

With the rifle they took some long shots at the dead glass disks on a signal tower far up the track, but nothing happened. When they were closer though, one of the signals suddenly swung up wildly alight, a burning color. Lawrence was about to take a shot at it when they heard the train behind them.

They slid down an embankment, through the bull nettle and bluebonnets, to walk a path along the bottom. When the freight train reached them, they turned to watch it go

by, and as one of the boxcars passed, Big Lawrence, holding the rifle against his hip, pumped five or six rounds into
the side of it. Against the thundering noise of the train, the
muted shots had no apparent connection with the violent
way the blood-red wood of the boxcar door burst out angling and splintered off all pine-white.

As they walked on, Lawrence looked at Harold, grinned,
and said: "Don't reckon there was any hoboes in it, do you?"
And Harold laughed.

Then they reached the trestle — a rickety-looking
wooden structure, like scaffolding, propped over a narrow
chalk-rock gully. They walked across it, balancing on the
rails.

"Maybe there won't be another one today," said Harold
when they reached the other side.

Lawrence nodded grimly. "There'll be another one," he
said. "Let's wait down at the hole."

Harold followed Lawrence along the culvert and down
into the creek hollow. They walked it in file, Lawrence
ahead, stepping around tall slaky rocks that pitched up
abruptly from the hot shale. Heat came out of this dry stone,
sharp as acid, wavering up in black lines. Then at a bend
before them was the water hole, small now and stagnant,
and they turned off to climb the bank in order to reach it
from the other side. Harold was in front now, and as they
came over the rise, he saw the rabbit first. Standing between two oak stumps ten feet in front of them, standing
up like a miniature kangaroo, ears winced back, looking
away, toward the railroad track. Then Lawrence saw it too,
and tried to motion Harold off with one hand, bringing his
rifle up quick with the other.

The sound came as one, but within one spurting circle of explosion, the two explosions were distinct.

"Goddam," said Lawrence, frowning. He walked slowly toward the stumps, then looked at Harold before he picked up the rabbit. *"Goddam it!"* he said through clenched teeth.

One side of the rabbit, from the stomach down, looked as though it had been pushed through a meat grinder.

"You must be crazy," Lawrence said. "Why didn't you let me git 'im, goddam it? I could've got him in the *head!*"

He dropped the rabbit across one of the stumps and stood scowling down at it.

Harold picked up the rabbit, studied it. "Sure tore hell out of it, didn't it?" he said.

Lawrence spat and turned away. Harold watched him for a minute walking down toward the water hole; then he draped the rabbit across the stump and followed.

They leaned the guns against the dry chalk rock that rose at their backs, and sat down. Harold brought out the cigarettes and offered them, so that Lawrence took one first, and then Harold. And Harold struck the match.

"Got the car tonight?" he asked, holding the light.

Big Lawrence didn't answer at once for drawing on the cigarette. "Sure," he said then, admitting, "but I've got a date." In this incredible sunlight, the flame of the match seemed colorless, only chemical, without heat.

"Where you gonna go?" Harold asked. "To the picture show?"

"I dunno," said Lawrence, watching the smoke. "Maybe I will."

The water hole was small, about ten feet across, over-hung only by a dwarfed sand willow on the other bank, so that all around the dead burning ground was flushed with sun, while one half of the hole itself cast back the scene in shimmering distortion.

Over and on the water now, in and through the shadow that fell half across them, played wasps and water spiders, dragonflies, snake doctors, and a thousand gray gnats. Then the hornet came — deep-ribbed and golden, whirring bright as a spinning coin; it hung in a hummingbird twist just on the water surface in the deepest shadow of the tree, and Lawrence threw a rock at it.

And an extraordinary thing happened. The hornet, rising frantically up through the willow branches, twisted once, and came down out of the tree in a wild whining loop, and lit exactly on the back of Harold's shirt collar, and then very deliberately, as Lawrence saw, crawled inside.

"Set still," said Lawrence, taking a handful of the shirt at the back and the hornet with it, holding it.

Harold had his throat arched out, the back of his neck scrunched away from the shirt collar. "Did you git it?" he kept asking.

"Set still, god dang it," said Lawrence, laughing, watching Harold's face from the side, before finally closing his hand on the shirt, making the hornet crackle as hard and dry as an old wooden penny-matchbox when he clenched his fist.

And then Lawrence had it out, in his hand, and they were both bent over it looking. It was dead now, wadded and broken. And in the shade of Lawrence's hand, the gold of the hornet had become as shoddy drab as the phosphorus dial at noon — it was the stinger, sticking out like a wire hair, taut in an electric quaver, that still lived.

"Look at that goddam thing," said Lawrence of the stinger, and made as if to touch it with his hand.

"Look out, you'll get stung," said Harold.

"Look at it," said Lawrence, intent.

"They all do that," Harold said.

"Sure, but not like that."

Lawrence flicked it with his finger, but nothing happened.

"Maybe we can get it to sting something," said Harold, and he tried to catch a doodlebug crawling on a bluebonnet that grew alone between them, but he missed it. So Lawrence bent the flower itself over, to get the stinger to penetrate the stem. "It'll kill it," he said. "It's acid."

Lawrence held the tail of the hornet tightly between his thumb and finger, squeezing to get more of the stinger out, until it came out too far and stopped moving — and Lawrence, still squeezing, slowly emptied the body of its white filling. Some of it went on his finger. Lawrence smelled it, then he let Harold smell it before he wiped his finger on the grass.

They each lit another cigarette. Big Lawrence threw the match in the water, and a minute after it had floated out, took up the .243, drew a bead, and clipped it just below the burnt head.

"Why?" he asked Harold, handing him the rifle. "Are you goin' to the show tonight?"

"I might," Harold said.

"Yeah, but have you got a date?"

"I reckon I could get one," said Harold, working the bolt.

"I've got one with Helen Ward," said Lawrence.

Harold sighted along the rifle.

"You know her sister?" Lawrence asked.

"Who, Louise?"

"Sure, maybe we could get 'em drunk."

Harold held his breath, steadying the rifle. Then he took a shot. "Sure I know her," he said.

They shot water targets, with the rifle, Harold using up the shots Lawrence owed him. Once, however, after he dug an old condensed-milk can out of the bank and sat it afloat on the water, Lawrence took up the shotgun and held the muzzle about a foot from the can.

"TNT," he said, and pulled the trigger. "Hot damn!"

They sat there for an hour, talking a little and smoking, shooting at crawfish and dragonflies, or underwater rocks that shone through flat yellow or, more often, dull dead brown.

Then they heard the train, the whistle, distant and ghostly.

"Come on," said Lawrence, tight-lipped.

They left the guns and climbed the bank up to the trestle — to the understructure of it, a labyrinthine tangle of creosote beams, crisscrossed and jutting out abruptly where it had been repaired and shored up over many years, the Tinkertoy work of a mad child.

Under the tracks now, they moved spiderlike through the angled beams toward the middle of the span. The whistle of the train sounded again, closer now — and, beneath their hands and feet, along their arms and legs, whenever their bodies touched the wood of the trestle, they felt the tremor of the approaching train.

At a point near the middle, where two beams crossed about four feet directly beneath the tracks, they stopped, crouching, each with one foot in the V where the beams bisected, their hands grasping the tie above them that separated the tracks. They could tell from the increasing tremor of the structure how much closer the train was — about the length of a football field — and now they could hear the train itself, the rumble of it, still distant, almost peaceful, like a drowsing bull.

Big Lawrence turned, his face flushed almost crimson, so that his grin was strangely incongruous. *"Don't fergit!"* he said.

"I won't," said Harold.

They waited a few seconds more . . . three, four, five . . . "Now!" said Lawrence, and they raised their heads up between the tracks so that their chins were resting on the tie.

Even before he looked at the train, Harold was aware how Lawrence, without turning his head, had cut his eyes over quickly to make sure that Harold's chin was on the railroad tie, the way it was supposed to be, thrusting forward, throat pressing into the wood — and his eyes open. In this position, the tops of their heads were about two inches higher than the rails themselves, and their faces toward the oncoming train.

What Harold saw was like a scene in a movie when the camera is shooting up at an angle from the floor, magnifying and distorting — the locomotive — now in extreme close-up, the lower part especially, the cowcatcher, seen as a gigantic black plowshare, appearing knife-pointed and razor-sharp. And then the sound of the train's whistle was an ear-shattering hysterical scream, but inside it, above it, came Lawrence's own scream: *"Don't fergit!"* And suddenly the train was on them, an unimaginably explosive eclipse.

Harold strained to keep his eyes open, because that was the thing, and it was what Big Lawrence had told him not to forget.

And afterward, it was the first thing Lawrence wanted to know. "Well, did you?"

"Yeah," said Harold, then added, "as long as I could . . . till the cinders got in 'em."

"Yeah," Lawrence admitted, "me too. Anyway, it's just the first part that counts — when it's comin' right for you, that's when it really counts."

"Yeah," Harold agreed, "that's when it really counts."

Or at least he said he agreed. It was not easy to disagree with Big Lawrence. Also he believed in his heart that Lawrence was probably right; if something was so scary that you didn't want to do it, then it must be worth doing. The whole idea, of course, had been Lawrence's. At first it had somehow seemed quite natural. They had been walking across the trestle, and when they heard the train coming, they started to climb down the side, at least enough to be well off the track.

"Wait a minute," Lawrence had said, taking hold of Harold's arm. "We don't have to git off yet. It ain't even in sight."

They had waited until the locomotive had come around the bend, about a hundred yards away.

"We'll make him blow the whistle first," said Lawrence, but the whistle was already shrieking, and the engineer peering ahead and shaking his fist.

Then, clinging to the crossbeam beneath the tracks, they had watched the train roar by overhead. That was when Lawrence got the notion of climbing high enough to put their heads up between the ties. The idea of keeping their eyes open to watch the train's horrific approach was fairly new, and this was only the second time they had tried that part of it. Harold was relieved that even Lawrence had not been able to keep his eyes open the whole time.

They climbed down from the trestle and went back to get their guns. Then when they passed near the stumps, Harold crossed over and picked up the dead rabbit, Lawrence watching him.

"What're you gonna do with that damn thing?" Lawrence asked, sounding angry.

"Aw I dunno," said Harold. "Might as well take it along."

Lawrence watched while Harold held it by the ears and kicked at a piece of newspaper, all twisted dry and yellow in the grass. He got the paper, shook it out straight, and he wrapped it around the rabbit.

They started across the field, Lawrence not talking for a while. Then they stopped to light a cigarette. "I got a good idea," Lawrence said, cradling the rifle to one arm. "We can cook it."

Harold didn't answer, but as they walked back toward the stumps, he looked at the sun.

"I wonder what time it is anyhow," he said.

Using Harold's pocketknife, Big Lawrence, after it was decided, sat on one of the stumps to skin the rabbit while Harold went pushing around through the Johnson grass, folding it aside with his feet, peering and picking up small dead branches, bundling them to build the fire.

At the stumps, Lawrence cursed the knife, tried the other blade, and sawed at the rabbit's neck, twisting the head in his hand.

"Couldn't cut hot nigger-piss," he said, but he managed

to tear the head off, and to turn the skin back on itself at the neck, so that he pulled it down over the body like a glove reversed on an unborn hand, it glistened so.

He had to stop with the skin halfway down to cut off the front feet, and in doing this, hacking once straight on from the point of the blade, the blade suddenly folded back against his finger. Grimacing, he opened the knife slowly, saying nothing, but he sucked at the finger and squeezed it between two others until, through all this heavy red of rabbit, sticking, covering his whole hand now, he could almost see, but never quite, where in one spot on his smallest finger, up through all the thick dark blood of the rabbit, he was bleeding too.

He went down to the water hole to wash his hands, but he finished skinning the rabbit first.

When he got back, Harold was bent over, ready to light the fire.

Then it was Lawrence who squinted at the sun, still monstrous but lower now in the western sky. "Well, are we goin' to the goddam picture show or not?" he demanded.

"I don't care," said Harold, looking up at him. "Do you want to?"

"Well, we better git back if we're goin'."

Harold pulled the old newspaper from where he had put it to start the fire. Then he wrapped it around the rabbit again, and he stuffed the whole thing inside his shirt. Finally he folded the skin square and put it in his back pocket, like a handkerchief.

Lawrence had the rabbit's head. He tried to get the eyes to stay open, and one did stay open, but only the white showed when he sat it on the stump. He took a rock from the windbreak Harold had built for the fire and put this on the stump, too, behind the head, and they started across the field. When they were a little way out, they took shots at the head, and finally Lawrence used the last of the shotgun shells he had coming to go up close and blast the head, and finally a part of the stump itself.

"Bombs away!" he said the last time he pulled the trigger, up close.

Before they reached the street where Lawrence lived, they could hear Tommy Sellers cursing and Crazy Ralph Wilton, farther, yelling: "All the way! All the way!" and as they turned in, Tommy Sellers was there, coming toward them, walking up the middle of the street, swinging his glove by one finger.

Harold pulled the wad of newspaper out of his shirt and held it up to show, and Tommy Sellers stopped and kicked around at a pile of dead grass in the gutter, while in the distance Crazy Ralph was yelling: "All the way! All the way!" Then Tommy Sellers found the ball with his foot, and, bending over, in a low twisting windup from the gutter, without once looking where, he threw it — and the ball lifted like a shot to hang sailing for an instant in a wide climbing arc toward the sun.

Big Lawrence brought his rifle off his shoulder. "Ka-*pow!* Ka-*pow!*" and the barrel point wavered, sighting up the lazy wake of the ball. "Dead-sonafabitch-bird," he said.

Tommy Sellers was standing closer now, hands on his hips, not seeing half a block away, where Crazy Ralph, with his eyes wild, his fingers nervously tapping the glove palm, was trying to pick the bouncing throw off the headlight of a parked car.

"Goddam that thing stinks!" said Lawrence, making a

face when Harold opened the newspaper. The paper had become like a half-dried cloth, stiff, or sticking in places and coming to pieces. Almost at once a fly was crawling over the chewed-up part of the rabbit.

"You know what it's like?" said Lawrence. "Rotten old afterbirth!" and he spat, seeming to retch slightly.

"What was it?" asked Tommy Sellers, looking closely at the rabbit, then up, not caring, dancing away to make an over-the-shoulder circus catch of the throw from Crazy Ralph.

As they walked on, Harold wrapped the newspaper around the rabbit again and put it in his shirt.

"It's already startin' to rot!" said Big Lawrence.

"Aw you're crazy," Harold said.

"*Crazy,*" repeated Lawrence through clenched teeth. "You're the one who's crazy. What'll you do . . . eat it?" He laughed, angrily, spitting again.

They were walking in the street now in front of Lawrence's house. Tommy Sellers and Ralph Wilton were at the curb, throwing their gloves up through the branches of a stunted cedar tree where the ball was caught.

There were some people standing around the steps at Lawrence's front porch. One was a young woman wearing an apron over her dress — and a little girl was holding on to the dress with both hands, pressing her face into the apron, swinging herself slowly back and forth, so that the woman stood braced, her feet slightly apart. She stroked the child's head with one hand, and in the other she was holding the dead cat.

They watched Harold and Lawrence in the street in front of the house. Once, the woman moved her head and spoke to the big man standing on the porch, who frowned without looking at her.

Harold didn't turn in with Lawrence. "See you at the picture show," he said.

As he walked on, the fall of their voices died past him.

"How'd it happen, Son?" he heard Lawrence's dad ask.

He turned off on a vacant lot that cut through toward the livery stable, where he would meet Les Newgate for his ride home. Halfway across, he pulled out the paper and opened it. He studied it, brought it up to his face, and smelled it. Then he put it back in the paper and inside his shirt. "Ain't nothin' better'n fried rabbit with biscuit an' gravy," his granddad always said.

VII

ON AN EAST TEXAS PRISON FARM, about two hundred miles away, a different kind of action was unfolding. Cap'n Jack, his cheek bulging with chaw, was shouting furiously: "Git 'im, Bull! Git that black son'bitch!"

And Bull Watson, 250 pounds, pig-bristle haircut, emptied his ten-gauge riot gun at the escaping prisoner, kicking out craters of red dirt on both sides of the man who scrambled over the culvert and up the ragged embankment.

A dozen other prisoners, all black or Mexican, cheered him on: "Go, Big Nail, go!"

"*Vamos, amigo!*"

"Big Nail gonna make it! Hot damn!"

And as the prisoner disappeared into the scrub-brush at the top of the embankment, Bull tried to avoid the Cap'n's glare of contempt.

"Ah may of gotta piece of 'im, Cap," said Bull.

"You got shit, that's what you got," said Cap. He spat a glittering brown trail of Red Man into the dust, then turned to the toothless Mexican trusty standing alongside

74

and pointed to the old pickup with the faded letters: TEXAS STATE PRISON SYSTEM.

"Go git the dogs!" he bellowed, "an' git Slim an' Dusty! Tell Warden Big Nail's makin' a run fer it!"

The trusty turned and headed for the truck, as the other yelled after him: "An' bring my Winchester!"

"If Warden don't want 'em runnin'," muttered Bull, "then how come ah can't use my thirty-thirty on the job?"

" 'Cause he don't want nobody gittin' killed, that's how come," said Cap, then spat and added quietly, "an' 'cause he's a goddam nigger-lover . . . now, jest shut your hole an' git on over yonder an' check them leg-irons."

Bull hitched up his trousers and headed toward the prisoners, while Cap pulled out his .357 Magnum and slowly cocked it.

"Awright," he said in a low snarl, "if they's anybody else wants to give ole Cap a little target practice" — he fired a deafening shot over their heads, causing them all to flinch — "he can jest start haulin' ass."

Across the culvert and beyond the embankment, Big Nail moved through the mesquite brush like a wounded animal, half hobbled by one leg-iron he had failed to slip.

"Big Nail be long gone from this place!" he said aloud. "Glory to the fuckin' Jesus!"

In the distance behind he could hear Cap'n ranting at the prisoners and he knew that the Mexican was not yet back with the dogs.

"Long gone now. Hot damn! Praise to the fuckin' Jesus!"

He ran without letup until he reached a narrow branch of the Cotton Mouth River — dried now in the raging heat to scarcely more than a rocky creekbed. But the water was deep enough to cover his feet.

"Well, shit-fire," he said. "And so long, hound-dog!" And he stepped carefully into the precious fluid and headed downstream.

With the afternoon sun filtering down from the treetops, Big Nail moved through the woods with his hobbled gait like a figure crossing the strobe-lit landscape of a horror film — a gaunt black hulk of a man whose knife-scarred face, even in repose, appeared set in a permanent scowl because one of his wounds had severed a facial muscle or two controlling his features. It was, however, an expression not inappropriate to his temperament, which was villainous in an almost absolute sense. It was as if he could no longer tell whether a hand was beating him or caressing him; he had become the dog that snarls while it is being fed.

When he emerged from the woods and the streaming dappled light, he had lost his pursuers. The distant dogs were silent, thwarted by the water-covered trail. But Big Nail's face showed no sign of gladness at that fact nor even relief; his eyes remained dead. Long ago something in him had been broken for good.

Back in the office at the prison farm, the Warden was reviewing the situation with Cap'n and Bull Watson. Under a trophy-size set of mounted antlers, the Warden sat at his desk, his feet with the new low-top customized Justins propped on a nearby chair for all to see. He considered himself a cut above Cap'n and Bull Watson so he did not chew Red Man but diligently smoked a whiskey-seasoned briar instead; his corduroy jacket had deerskin elbow patches and a shooter's pad on the right shoulder.

"Warden, I'll tell you one thing," Bull Watson was saying, "that nigger would've been in two pieces right now if I had my thirty-thirty on the job."

The Warden gave him a sad, reproachful look. "Well, that's as fuckin' may be, Bull, but the plain fact of the matter is that if you missed him with a goddam scattergun, how in God's great name could you have hit him with a rifle?"

He looked over to Cap'n for confirmation. Cap'n took out an empty coffee can that he carried in his jacket pocket for the purpose and spat a mouthful of brown Red Man juice into it, before giving Bull a straight look.

"Reckon Warden's got a point there, Bull," he said, but then backed off a little. " 'Course now you wudn't aiming to kill 'im with that ten-gauge, was you?"

"Why hell no," said Bull, as if they should both know better. "I was jest tryin' to take off a foot or somethin'. Jest somethin' to slow 'im down. He was *movin'*, Warden." Then he added: "I still think I may have got a piece of him."

Warden tapped his pipe bowl into an ashtray with a show of strained patience. "Well now, Bull, be that as it fuckin' well may be. But Cap'n here says there weren't no blood found at the scene. None whatsofuckin'ever. Now in light of your theory that presents somethin' of a mystery, wouldn't you say?"

"Well, Warden, like I say, he was movin' faster than a northbound mail train." He forced a small chuckle. "Hell, I don't think he had *time* to bleed."

The other two failed to see the humor.

"I was sure hoping," said Warden, "that we could git 'im back here before it makes the Fort Worth news-wire.

It ain't exactly the kinda Pee-R we need jest now. But seein' as who it is, him bein' so goddam mean an' crazy, I reckon we better put out a all-points on 'im." He turned to Cap'n as if he were addressing a child. "You think you can handle that?"

"Yessir, Warden," said Cap'n briskly, trying to introduce an element of military smartness, in the hope it might distance him from the errant Bull Watson; and he got up to go and do it.

"But I'll tell you one thing, Warden," he felt obliged to add. "I'd jest bet he don't git too far — not wearin' that leg-iron."

"Yep," said Warden, "that's as may be. But if I know Big Nail, he'll probly git far enough to make *somebody's* worst nightmare come true."

VIII

HAROLD came into the open-end, dirt-floor shed where C.K. was sitting on the ground against the wall, reading a *Western Story* magazine.

The boy was carrying a pillowcase that was bunched out at the bottom, about a third filled with something, and C.K. looked up and smiled.

"What you doin', Hal — bringin' in the crop?"

Harold walked on over to one side of the shed where the kindling was stacked and pulled down an old sheet of newspaper, which he shook out to double-page size and spread in front of them. He dumped the gray-grass contents of the pillowcase onto the paper, and then straightened up to stand with his hands on his hips, frowning down at it.

C.K. was looking at it, too; but he was laughing — in his sometimes soft and almost soundless way, shaking his head as though this surely might be the final irony. "Sho' is a lotta gage," he said.

He reached out a hand and rolled a dry pinch of it between his thumb and forefinger.

"You reckon it's dried out enough?" Harold asked, as he

squatted down opposite. "I don't wantta leave it out there no more — not hangin' on that sycamore, anyway — it's beginnin' to look funny hangin' up out there." He glanced past the end of the shed toward the farmhouse that was about thirty yards away. "Heck, Dad's been shootin' dove down in there all week — an' this mornin' that ole hound of Les Newgate's was runnin' round with a piece of it in his mouth. I had to get it away from 'im 'fore they seen it."

C.K. took another pinch of it and briskly crushed it between his flat palms, then held them up, cupped, smelling it.

"They wouldn't of knowed what it was noway," he said.

"You crazy?" said Harold. "You think my dad don't know locoweed when he sees it?"

"Don't look much like no locoweed now, though, do it?" said C.K., flatly, raising expressionless eyes to the boy.

"He's seen it dried out, too, I bet," said Harold, loyal, sullen, turning away.

"Sho' he is," said C.K., weary and acid. "Sho', ah bet he done blow a lot of it too, ain't he? Sho', why ah bet you daddy one of the biggest ole hopheads in Texas! Why ah bet you he smoke it an' eat it an' jest anyway he can git it into his ole haid! Hee-hee!" He laughed at the mischievous image. "Ain't that right, Hal?"

"You crazy?" demanded Harold, frowning fiercely. He took C.K.'s wrist. "Lemme smell it," he said.

He drew back after a second.

"I can't smell nothin' but your dang sweat," he said.

" 'Course not," said C.K., frowning in his turn, and brushing his hands, "you got to git it jest when the flower break — that's the boo-kay of the plant, you see, that's what we call that."

"Do it again," said Harold.

"Ah ain't goin' to do it again," said C.K., peevishly, closing his eyes for a moment, ". . . it's a waste on you — ah do it again, you jest say you smell my sweat. You ain't got the nose for it noway — you got to know you business 'fore you start foolin' round with this plant."

"I can do it, C.K.," said the boy earnestly. "Come on, dang it."

C.K. sighed elaborately and selected another small bud from the pile.

"Awright now, when ah rub it in my hand," he said sternly, "you let out you breath — then ah cup my hand, you put you nose in an' smell strong. You got to suck in strong through you nose!"

They did this.

"You smell it?" asked C.K.

"Yeah, sort of," said Harold, leaning back again.

"That's the boo-kay of the plant — they ain't no smell like it."

"It smells like tea," said the boy.

"Well, now that's why they calls it that, you see — but it smell like somethin' else too."

"What?"

"Like mighty fine gage, that's what."

"Well, whatta you keep on callin' it that for?" Harold wanted to know. "That ain't what that Mex'can called it — he called it 'pot.' "

"That ole Mex," said C.K., brushing his hands and laughing, "he sho' were funny, weren't he? . . . thought he could pick cotton . . . told me he used to pick-a-bale-a-day. Ah had to laugh when he say that . . . oh, sho', he call it lotta things. He call it 'baby,' too. He say: 'Man,

don't forget the baby now!' He mean bring a few sticks of
it out to the field, you see, that's what he mean by that.
He call it 'charge,' too. Sho'. Them's slang names. Them
names git started people don't want the po-lice, nobody like
that, to know they business, you see what ah mean? They
make up them names, go on an' talk about they business
nobody know what they sayin', you see what ah mean?"

He stretched his legs out comfortably and crossed his
hands over the magazine that was still in his lap.

"Yes, indeed," he said after a minute, staring at the pile
on the newspaper, and shaking his head. "Ah tell you right
now, boy — that sho' is a lotta gage."

Harold picked some up and crumpled it.

"You reckon it's dried out enough?" he asked again.

C.K. took out his sack of Bull Durham.

"Well ah tell you what we goin' have to do," he said with
genial authority, ". . . we goin' have to test it."

He slipped two cigarette papers from the attached packet,
one of which he licked and placed alongside the other,
slightly overlapping it.

"Ah use two of these papers," he explained, concentrating on the work. "That give us a nice slow-burnin' stick,
you see."

He selected a small segment from the pile and crumpled
it, letting it sift down from his fingers into the cupped cigarette paper; and then he carefully rolled it, licking his pink-
white tongue slowly over the whole length of it after it was
done. "Ah do that," he said, "that shut it in good, you see."
And he held it up for them both to look at; it was much
thinner than an ordinary cigarette, and still glittering with
the wet of his tongue.

"That cost you half-a-dollah in Dallas," he said, staring at it.

"Shoot," said the boy, uncertain.

"Sho' would," said C.K., ". . . oh you git three fo' a dollah, you know the man. 'Course that's mighty good gage ah talkin' 'bout you pay half-a-dollah . . . that' you *quality* gage. Ah don't know how good quality this here is yet, you see."

He lit it.

"Sho' smell good though, don't it."

Harold watched him narrowly as he wafted the smoking stick back and forth beneath his nose.

"Taste mighty good too. Shoot, ah jest bet this is ver' good quality gage. You wantta taste of it?" He held it out.

"Naw, I don't want none of it right now," said Harold. He got up and walked over to the kindling stack, and drew out from a stash there a package of Camels; he lit one, returned the pack to its place, and came back to sit opposite C.K. again.

"Yeah," said C.K. softly, gazing at the thin cigarette in his hand, "ah feel this gage awready . . . this is fine."

"What does it feel like?" asked Harold.

C.K. had inhaled again, very deeply, and was holding his breath, severely, chest expanded like a person who is learning to float, his dark brow slightly knit in the effort of working at it physically.

"It feel *fine*," he said at last, smiling.

"How come it jest made me sick that time?" asked the boy.

"Why, ah tole you, Hal," said C.K. impatiently. " 'Cause you tried to fight against it, that's why . . . you tried to fight that gage, so it jest make you sick. Sho', that was good gage that ole Mex had."

"Shoot, all I felt, 'fore I got sick, was jest right dizzy."

C.K. had taken another deep drag and was still holding it, so that now when he spoke, casually but without exhaling, it was from the top of his throat, and his voice sounded odd and strained: "Well, that's 'cause you mind is young an' unformed, you see . . . that gage jest come into you mind an' cloud it over!"

"My mind?" said Harold.

"Sho', you *brain!*" said C.K. in a whispery rush of voice as he let out the smoke. "You brain is young an' unformed, you see . . . that smoke come in, it got nowhere to go, it jest cloud you young brain over!"

Harold flicked his cigarette a couple of times.

"I reckon it's as good as any dang nigger-brain," he said after a minute.

"Now boy, don't mess with me," said C.K., frowning, ". . . you ast me somethin' an' ah tellin' you. You brain is young an' unformed . . . it's all smooth, you brain, smooth as that piece of shoe leather. That smoke jest come in an' cloud it over." He took another drag. "Now you take somebody old as I is," he said in his breath-holding voice, "with a full-growed brain, it ain't smooth — it's got all ridges in it, all over, go this way an' that. Shoot, a man know what he doin' he have that smoke runnin' up one ridge an' down the other. He con-trol his high, you see what ah mean, he don't fight 'gainst it . . ." His voice died away in the effort of holding breath and speaking at the same time — and, after exhaling again, he finished off the cigarette in several quick little drags, then broke open the butt with lazy care and emptied the few remaining bits from it back onto the pile. *"Yeah . . . ,"* he said, almost inaudibly, an absent smile on his lips.

Harold sat or half reclined, though somewhat stiffly, supporting himself with one arm, just staring at C.K. for a moment before he shifted a little to one side, flicking his cigarette. "Shoot," he said, "I just wish you'd tell me what it feels like, that's all."

C.K., though he was sitting cross-legged now with his back against the side of the shed, gave the appearance of substance without bone, like a softly filled sack that has slowly, imperceptibly sprawled and found its final perfect contour, while his head lay back against the shed, watching the boy out of half-closed eyes. He laughed softly.

"Boy, ah done tole you," he said in a voice like a whisper, "it feel *good!*"

"Well, that ain't nothin', dang it," said Harold. "I awready feel good!"

"Uh-huh," said C.K. with dreamy finality.

"Well, I do, god dang it," said Harold, glaring at him.

"That's right," said C.K., nodding, closing his eyes, and they were both silent for a few minutes, until C.K. looked at the boy again and spoke as though there had been no pause at all. "But you don't feel as good now as you do at you birthday though, do you? Like when right after you daddy give you that twenty-two rifle? An' then you don't feel as *bad* as the time he was whuppin' you for shootin' that doe with it neither, do you? Yeah. Well now that's how much difference they is, you see, between that cigarette you got in you hand an' the one ah jest put out. Now that's what ah tellin' you."

"Shoot," said Harold, flicking his half-smoked Camel and then mashing it out on the ground. "You're crazy."

C.K. laughed. "Sho' ah is," he said.

They fell silent again, C.K. appearing almost asleep, humming to himself, and Harold sitting opposite, frowning down to where his own finger traced lines without pattern in the dirt floor of the shed.

"Where we gonna keep this stuff at, C.K.?" he demanded finally, his words harsh and reasonable. "We can't jest leave it sittin' out like this."

C.K. seemed not to have heard, or perhaps simply to consider it without opening his eyes; then he did open them, and when he leaned forward and spoke, it was with a fresh and remarkable cheerfulness and clarity: "Well now, the first thing we got to do is to clean this gage. We got to git them seeds outta there an' all them little branches. But the ver' first thing we do" — and he reached into the pile — "is to take some of this here flower, these here ver' small leaves, an' put them off to the side. That way we got us two kinds of gage, you see — we got us a light gage an' a heavy gage."

He started breaking off the stems and taking them out, Harold joining in after a while; and then they began crushing the dry leaves with their hands.

"How we ever gonna git all them dang seeds outta there?" asked Harold.

"Now ah show you a trick 'bout that," said C.K., smiling and leisurely getting to his feet. "Where's that pilly-cover at?"

He spread the pillowcase flat on the ground and, lifting the newspaper, dumped the crushed leaves on top of it. Then he folded the cloth over them and kneaded the bundle with his fingers, pulverizing it. After a minute of this, he opened it up again, flat, so that the pile was sitting on the pillowcase now as it had been before on the newspaper.

"You hold on hard to that end," he told Harold, and he took the other himself and slowly raised it, tilting it, and agitating it. The round seeds started rolling out of the pile, down the taut cloth and onto the ground. C.K. put a corner of the pillowcase between his teeth and held the opposite corner out with one hand; then, with his other hand, he tapped gently on the bottom of the pile, and the seeds poured out by the hundreds, without disturbing the rest.

"Where'd you learn that at, C.K.?" asked Harold.

"Shoot, you got to know you business you workin' with this plant," said C.K., ". . . waste our time pickin' out them ole seeds." He stood for a moment looking around the shed. "Now we got to have us somethin' to keep this gage in — we got to have us a box, somethin' like that, you see."

"Why can't we jest keep it in that?" asked Harold, referring to the pillowcase.

C.K. frowned. "Naw, we can't keep it in that," he said. "Keep it in that like ole sacka turnip . . . we got to git us somethin' — a nice little box, somethin' like that, you see. How 'bout one of you empty shell-boxes?"

"They ain't big enough," said Harold.

C.K. resumed his place, sitting and slowly leaning back against the wall, looking at the pile again.

"They sho' ain't, is they," he said, happy with the fact.

"We could use three or four of 'em," Harold said.

"Wait a minute now," said C.K., "we talkin' here, we done forgit 'bout this heavy gage." He laid his hand on the smaller pile, as though to reassure it. "One of them shell-boxes do fine for that — an' ah tell you what we need for this light gage now ah think of it . . . is one of you momma's quart fruit-jars."

"Shoot, I can't fool around with them dang jars, C.K.," said the boy.

C.K. made a little grimace of impatience.

"You momma ain't grudge you one of them fruit-jars, Hal — she ast you 'bout it, you jest say it got broke. No, you say you done use that jar put you fishin'-minners in it. Hee-hee . . . she won't even wantta see that jar no more, you tell her that."

"I ain't gonna fool around with them jars, C.K."

C.K. sighed and started rolling another cigarette.

"Ah jest gonna twist up a few of them sticks now," he explained, "an' put them off to the side."

"When're you gonna smoke some of that other?" asked Harold.

"What, that heavy gage?" said C.K., raising his eyebrows as in surprise at the suggestion. "Shoot, that ain't no workin'-hour gage there, that you *Sunday* gage . . . oh you mix a little bit of that into you light gage now and then you feel like it — but you got to be sure nobody goin' to mess with you 'fore you turn that gage full on . . . 'cause you jest wanna lay back then an' take it easy." He nodded to himself in agreement with this, his eyes intently watching his fingers work the paper. "You see . . . you don't *swing* with you heavy gage, you jest *goof* . . . that's what you call that. Now you light gage, you swing with you light gage . . . you con-trol that gage, you see. Say a man have to go out an' work, why he able to *enjoy* that work. Like now you seen me turn on some of this light gage, didn't you? Well, ah may have to go out with you daddy a little later on an' string that fence wire, or work with my posthole digger, with my light gage on. Sho', that's you sociable gage, you light gage is — this here other, this heavy, well, that's what you call you *thinkin'* gage . . . hee-hee. Shoot, I wouldn't wantta even see no posthole digger I turn that gage full on!"

He rolled the cigarette up, slowly, licking it with great care.

"Yeah," he said half-aloud, ". . . ole fruit-jar be fine for this light gage." He chuckled. "That way we jest look right in there, know how much we got on hand at all time."

"We got enough, I reckon," said Harold, understating his view.

"Sho' is," said C.K. "More'n the law allows at that."

"Is it against the law then sure enough, C.K.?" asked Harold in eager interest. "Like that Mex-can kept sayin' it was?"

C.K. gave a soft laugh.

"Ah jest reckon it is," he said, ". . . it's against all kinda law — what we got here is. Sho', they's one law say you can't have *none* of it, they put you in the jailhouse you do . . . then they's another law say they catch you with more than this much" — he reached down and picked up a handful to show — "well, then you in real trouble. Sho', you got more than that, why they say: 'Now this man got more gage than he need for his personal use, he must be sellin' it!' Then they say you a 'pusher.' That's what they call that, an' boy ah mean they put you way back in the jailhouse then!" He gave Harold a severe look. "Ah don't wanna tell you you business, you unnerstan' what ah mean, Hal, but like ah say, ah wudn't let on 'bout this to nobody — not to you frien' Big Law'ence or any of them people."

"Heck, don't you think I know better than to do that?"

Harold spat, looking away, as though surprised that the thought could have occurred.

C.K. resumed his work, rolling the cigarettes, and Harold watched him for a few minutes and then stood up.

"I reckon I could get a fruit-jar outta the cellar," he said, "if she ain't awready brought 'em up for her cannin'."

"That sho' would be fine, Hal," said C.K., without raising his head, licking the length of another thin stick of it. "Git two of 'em if you can."

When Harold came back with the fruit-jars and the empty shell-box, they transferred the two piles into them.

"How come it's against the law if it's so all-fired good?" he wanted to know.

"Well now, ah used to study that myself," said C.K., tightening the lid of the fruit-jar and giving it a pat. He laughed. "It ain't 'cause it make young boys like you sick, ah tell you that much."

"Well, what the heck is it then?"

C.K. put the fruit-jars beside the shell-box, placing them neatly, arranging them just so, in front of him, and seeming to consider the question while he was doing it.

"Ah tell you what it is," he said then, "it's 'cause a man see too much when he git high, that's what. He see right through everthing . . . you understan' what ah say?"

"What the heck are you talkin' about?"

"Well, maybe you too young to know what ah talkin' 'bout — but ah tell you they's a lotta trickin' an' lyin' go on in the world . . . they's a lotta ole bull-crap go on in the world . . . well, a man git high, he see right through all them tricks an' lies, an' all that ole bull-crap. He see right through there into the truth of it."

"Truth of what?"

"Everything."

"Dang you sure talk crazy, C.K."

"Sho', they got to have it 'gainst the law. Shoot, ever'-body git high, wouldn't be nobody git up an' feed the chickens. Hee-hee . . . everybody jest lay in bed. Jest lay in bed till they ready to git up. Sho', you take a man high on good gage, he got no use for they ole bull-crap, 'cause he done see through there. Shoot, he lookin' right down into his very soul."

"I ain't never heard nobody talk so dang crazy, C.K."

"Well, you young, Hal — you goin' hear plenty crazy talk 'fore you is a growed man."

"Shoot."

"Now we got to think of us a good place to put this gage," he said, "a secret place. Where you think, Hal?"

"How 'bout that old smokehouse out back — ain't nobody goes in there."

"Shoot, that's a good place for it, Hal — you sure they ain't goin' tear it down no time soon?"

"Heck no, what would they tear it down for?"

C.K. laughed. "Yeah, that's right," he said. "Well, we take it out there after it git dark."

They fell silent, sitting together in the early afternoon. Through the open end of the shed the bright light had inched across the dirt floor till now they were both sitting half in the soft full sunlight.

"Ah jest wish ah knowed whether or not you daddy gonna work on that south-quarter fence today," said C.K. after a while.

"Aw, him and Les Newgate went over to Dalton," said Harold. "Heck, I bet they ain't back 'fore dark." Then he added: "You think we oughtta go down to the tank?"

91

C.K. appeared to give it judicious thought, although brief.

"Ah think we do awright today," he said glancing out at the blue sky and sniffing the air a little, ". . . shoot, we try some pork rind over at the second log — that's jest where he be 'bout now."

"We oughtta git started then," said Harold. "Reckon we can jest leave that dang stuff here till dark . . . we can stick it back behind that firewood."

"Sho'," said C.K., "we stick it back in there for the time bein' — an' ah think ah twist up one or two more these 'fore we set out . . . put a taste of this heavy in 'em." He laughed as he unscrewed the lid of the fruit-jar. "Shoot, this sho' be fine for fishin'," he said, ". . . ain't nothin' like good gage give a man the strength of patience — you want me to twist up one for you, Hal?"

Harold sighed. "Okay, but you lemme *lick* it, C.K."

C.K. smiled, starting to twist up another. "Sho'," he said softly, "that ain't gonna hurt it none."

IX

LATE EVENING and the farmhouse stood dark against the horizon, only one light burning in a room near the back.

Big Nail knelt in the shadow of the back porch listening intently for a long moment before creeping on all fours to the window and peering in. In the soft circle of lamplight from a table near the bed he could see the middle-aged couple lying there — the woman asleep with her hair up in curlers and he reading a folded newspaper. Sitting on the table, next to the lamp, was a small radio, dial glowing and fiddle music softly playing. It was "The Texas Farm and Home Program" from Waco, featuring country-and-western music, interspersed with market reports on the latest price of livestock and with special forecasts of corn and cotton futures. The music was being performed by W. Lee "Pappy" O'Daniel and his Hillbilly Boys. They were singing:

> "Ah like mountain music
> Good ole mountain music
> Played by a real hillbilly band."

Crouched in the shadows, only a few feet away, Big Nail was scarcely aware of the music, as the fingers of his right hand slowly uncovered a large heavy rock in the soft earth beneath the window.

> "Ah love that country rhythm
> Ah jest play right with 'em
> It's jest the bestest band what am."

In the bed the woman stirred and raised a hand to her head. The man mistook her gesture.

"I'm finished," he said, "if that's what you're about to start up on . . ." He dropped the folded newspaper to the floor and switched off the table lamp. "I reckon you want the radio off too."

She gave an elaborate sigh. "Leroy, that ain't what I was gonna say. I was *gonna* say that I felt right uneasy tonight."

"How come?"

"Well, I *don't know* how come." Her impatience had turned to irritation. "But would you please leave the radio on? It's a comfort."

The man grunted. "Well, jest don't leave it on all goddam night," he said, and he pulled his pillow on top of his head and went straight to sleep — indeed so quickly that he failed to hear the creak of the board at the sill of the bedroom door.

"Roy," his wife whispered suddenly, "there's somethin' . . ."

But Roy did not stir. And there was no more sound, except the radio's drone, until his wife screamed at the top of her voice: "Oh my God! Roy! Where's the gun at? Roy!"

With only the orange glow from the radio dial illuminating the room, events there were seen in the most obscure

and unreal way — predominantly the horrific countenance
of Big Nail, moving inexorably closer, and very fast, yet
caught up for a terrible instant, highlighted in the radio-
glow by a thousand beads of perspiration. The woman also
moved quickly and was half out of the bed when the first
blow of the rock in Big Nail's hand struck her behind the
ear with tremendous force, the heavy rock that then struck
the man still in bed time and time again.

And the nasal twang of "Pappy" O'Daniel was unre-
lenting:

> "Ah've heard Hi-wah-yans play
> In the land of Wicky-Wacky
> But ah must say
> They can't beat 'Turkey in the
> Straw,' by cracky."

Later that same year, "Pappy" O'Daniel ran for gover-
nor of Texas and was elected by a landslide.

X

USING a rusty tire-iron, C.K. slowly pried the old corral fence-board, weathered and broken, away from the post, which creaked and groaned as the nails were gradually wrenched out of the hardwood post that had held the board for so many years.

Farther along the fence, Harold was attempting to remove another board, by executing a series of whirling karate type back-kicks in its direction.

Having taken off one board, C.K. picked up another one-by-six, aged but sound, and started nailing it in place. While he hammered he sang one abrupt verse, Paul Robeson style:

> "Dere ain't no ham-mah
> Dat can ringa like mine, boy . . ."

Harold, having successfully connected with one of his kicks, yelled over at C.K.: "Hey, C.K.! Look! *Kay*-rotty de-fence! Aiee-ee!"

He attempted another whirling kick to demonstrate his technique on a broken section of fence-board, missed, and fell down in a graceless fashion.

"Dang it," he said and got up quickly, brushing himself off.

C.K. laughed. "Say 'Kay-whut kinda rotty fence'? Hee-hee . . . look like you 'Kay' ain't no good 'gainst this rotty ole fence, hee-hee-hee!"

He resumed hammering and singing, while Harold glared at him, before blurting out: "You can't sing worth a dang, C.K.! What kinda dumbell old nigger-song is that anyhow?"

C.K. looked at him with half-closed eyes and assumed a mockingly supercilious tone: "Well, that there jest happen to be a ver' famous ole Negra-song — sung by famous ole Negra slaves . . . all obah dis worl'.'"

Harold, still rubbing his knee, didn't laugh. "I reckon you think you're bein' smart, don't you?"

And C.K. got slightly annoyed in turn.

"No," he said quietly, "but ah tell you what ah do think — ah think we bettah git on with this fence patching 'fore you daddy come out an' start kickin' ass — namely, you ass an' mine!"

Harold frowned darkly. "Dang it, sometime I can't believe how crazy you are! Now watch this and learn something! This is Kung Fu *Kay*-rotty, a really old and ancient art of defense."

He took a careful stance, and tried the kick again.

"Aiee-eee!"

This time he managed to connect, and knocked off a dangling piece of the rotten fence-board.

"See there," he said, brushing his hands, " '*Kay*-rotty *de*-fense!' That's what they call that! I'll show you how to do it some time."

"Awright," said C.K., "ah could use myself some good *de*-fense."

"Yeah," said Harold with a short laugh, "you ain't just a'wolfin' you could — from what I hear tell."

"Say what?"

"You heard me."

"Ah hear you tryin' to *signify* somethin' you don't know what you tryin' to signify — that's what ah hear."

"Yeah, well I heard that you're still messin' aroun' with somebody else's woman — namely, Big Nail's!"

C.K.'s eyes widened in mock astonishment. "Cora Lee Lawson? Where you hear that?"

"Aw come on, C.K., everybody says that."

"Well, ah don't know you 'Mistuh *Everbody*,' but he be 'Mistuh *Wrongbody*,' he say that. Ah ain't study that with Cora Lee — she fambily. Ah take care her boy, Booker, that's what ah do. Booker be 'bout you age, Hal, he like my brother. He a good boy — you meet him someday. Shoot, ah think you like ole Booker. Anyhow, me an' Cora Lee be nobody business but us."

"Well, I just think you must be crazy to mess aroun' with her, after he's awready killed somebody for doin' it."

"Uh-huh, well, like ah say, you don't have to study none 'bout that, 'cause you don't know what you talkin' 'bout."

"Well, how come they call him 'Big Nail' anyhow?"

" 'Cause before he own a knife or a razor, he carry a sixty-penny nail — he use that 'stead of a knife . . ."

"Is that what he used to kill that guy with?"

"No, by that time he be usin' his razor."

Harold was impressed. "Dang, he must sure be tough."

C.K. chuckled. "He ain't tough, he jest ugly."

"Uh-huh," said Harold at his most skeptical. "Well, I sure wouldn't want to tangle with him."

C.K. smiled. "Well, ah jest don't think you ever be called on to do so, my man."

"An' neither should you," added Harold in an instant of concern.

"Ah reckon not," said C.K. almost absently.

Harold's new calf wandered out of the barn and into the corral.

"How come you' calf ain't out to pasture?" asked C.K.

"I brung 'im in to weigh him — shoot, I bet he's gained a full pound, maybe two, since yesterday. I'm gonna take him over later on an' weigh 'im on Les Newgate's cotton scale."

C.K. stopped working, walked across to the calf, and looked at it. "Yep, he puttin' it on awright . . ." He carefully encircled the calf's chest with his arms and lifted it.

"How much you think he weighs now?" asked Harold.

"Ah say sebenty, sebenty-five . . ."

"Lemme see." Harold went over and, with much greater effort, lifted the calf.

"Dang!" said Harold, lowering it, "feels like more than that to me! Feels more like a sack of feed — they weigh a hunnert."

"Well, that's jest 'cause you cain't git no good grip on a calf, you see, an' you usin' different muscle to lift, that's all that is."

They returned to their work. "Shoot," said Harold, "I just bet you anything he weighs more than seventy-five pounds."

"Maybe," said C.K., then smiled, sly and mischievous. "Now ah tell you a secret, Hal — 'bout how you can use this calf to win a lotta money an' *im*-press all you friends, an' all you fambly."

Harold stared at the calf. "What the heck are you talkin' about now, C.K.?"

"Awright, you know how you done lift that calf off the ground jest now?"

"Yeah."

"Well now you is a strong boy, Hal, an' you gonna git stronger. All you gotta do is lift that calf one time ever day."

"Huh?"

"Now say this calf gain one pound weight by this time tomorrow, you still be able to lift it, ain't that right? I mean, you be able to lift jest one more pound, ain't that right?"

"One more pound? Heck yes."

"An' next day, too — you be able to lift that calf if it just weigh one more pound than day before."

"Uh-huh."

"An' you be able to lift that calf ever day it weigh only one more pound than the last time you lift it — you unnerstan' what I say?"

"Yes, dang it!"

"Awright, say that calf gain one pound weight ever day an' you liftin' it off the ground ever day — in about two year' time you be liftin' a eight-hunnert-pound *steer!* Now what you think 'bout that?"

"Huh?"

C.K. assumed a dramatic stance. "That's right," he proclaimed in an announcer's voice, "you, Hal W. Stevens, be the first man in history able to lift a eight-hunnert-pound steer clean off the ground! Shoot, Hal, we make us some good money on this if you keep at it! Hee-hee!"

Harold, annoyed at having been tricked, stared at C.K. with a look of infinite exasperation.

"You keep at it, you're gonna get somethin' you ain't lookin' for . . ."

C.K. laughed. "Like what? Some of you rotty ole Kung-fence-Fu? Hee-hee-hee . . ."

"You'll see," said Harold grimly.

C.K. stared at him thoughtfully for a moment.

"You know what you got to do, Hal — ah mean aside from liftin' this calf ever day — you got to work on you sense of huma'."

"My what?"

"You don't know what sense of huma' is?" Contorting his face, he went through a series of laughs: "Hee-hee-hee . . . ho-ho-ho . . . har-har-har . . . see what ah mean?"

Harold glared at him, hopeless. "Will you jest git on with what you're suppose to be doin' and stop playin' the dang fool."

"Yessuh, massaboss," said C.K., and he resumed hammering and singing, while Harold continued to glare before going back to practice his ancient art of manly defense.

XI

THE FAIRGROUNDS, where the Big Red Onion was held, were devoid of any permanent buildings except for the Pavilion — a big shed, open on all sides, with rows of folding chairs, and a platform stage at one end. It was a place where prayer meetings were frequently held by the Holy Roller people. Before these meetings, mattresses would be stacked alongside the Pavilion, and members of the congregation who lost consciousness during the service would be carried outside and placed on one of the mattresses, there to recover their senses in the cool of the evening under a haze of Texas stars. During the Onion, however, families would spread blankets on the grass and sit there all day, listening to the country music played inside, while eating fried chicken, and drinking iced tea from a thermos.

Members of the family would occasionally leave the blanket and go over to the exhibitions of livestock and produce. For the children, the carnival midway — with its rides and fortune-tellers, its weight guessers, alligator woman, and cotton candy — was the important thing. The children would abandon the family blanket and not be seen again until after dark, when they returned, limp with exhaustion.

The preparations that went into the Onion, as seen from afar — hammering the stakes, raising the tents, stringing the banners and lights — did not seem related to that moment of sheer magic, when, on the first night, the car or truck reached that curve in the highway where it all suddenly came into view — like a night mirage, in blazing color . . . and with the vision came the sound — the calliope, that miraculous music of the spheres, associated exclusively with this ambiance where hours were no longer measured in minutes, but in the number of times on the Ferris wheel, the roller coaster, and the all-new, and terrifying, Loop-O-Plane, which not only swung the rider upside down at great speed, but simultaneously around and around — as though inside a spinning top being twisted on a vertical string.

At the entrance to the midway, Harold and Big Lawrence bought two cones of cotton candy and a cup of frozen custard. They proceeded to eat them in the traditional manner: a bit of cotton candy, which was then wrapped around the custard on the tongue.

The first game of chance they encountered was the hoop stand, where, cotton candy and custard in hand, they watched the people try to toss ten-inch wooden hoops over valuable prizes, the centerpiece of which was a chrome-plated, pearl-handled .45 pistol, with a crisp new fifty-dollar bill stuck in the barrel. The dapper man who ran the concession demonstrated again and again how easily it could be done, practically without looking, sometimes tossing the hoops over his shoulder, each to encircle a diamond ring, a gold watch, or the fabulous silver six-gun itself, and he maintained a spirited patter all the while: "Well now you don't have to play for the Fort Worth Cats to win yourself a very valuable prize," he chanted to the small crowd. "Any man, woman, or very small child can do it . . . this mornin' a little lady won herself a five-hunnert-dollar engagement ring, an' now she's lookin' for a cowboy to slip it on her finger . . . ten cents a hoop, six for a half, thirteen for a one-dollar bill . . . everybody's a winner today."

Big Lawrence snorted. "I think you're switchin' the dang hoops," he said querulously, after losing about a dollar. "I bet you're usin' a bigger one than we are." He flourished the hoop he had in his hand. "I bet this one won't *fit over* that dang gun!"

For a moment the hoop-man seemed genuinely amused by this notion. "Well, young man, would you like to make a ten-dollar bet on that advanced theory of yours?"

"No," said Lawrence, "but I'm gonna see for myself," and he started to climb over the counter, which, at chest height, seemed designed to make this difficult.

"No one allowed beyond the toss-line," said the hoop-man, and he snatched the hoop out of Lawrence's hand, "but I'll be glad to prove it for you." And, turning away, he adroitly tossed Lawrence's hoop directly over the pistol.

"He could've switched it right then!" said Lawrence, looking to Harold and the others. "When he turned away like that he could've switched it right then!"

This idea did not go without acceptance by several in the crowd, who murmured knowingly — and something might have come of it, except that, as if on cue, a woman with a roadhouse hairdo, who had been leaning against the counter all along, and who had tossed a hoop from time to time to no avail, suddenly, but somehow laconically, tossed one that, as the hoop-man was quick to proclaim, was now encircling *a solid gold bracelet!*"

He plucked the bracelet from the peg and presented it to her with a flourish. "Young lady, this must be your lucky day!"

"But how do I know it's really gold?" she asked, looking from the hoop-man to two or three nearest her in the crowd.

"Well now, that's a fair question," said the hoop-man, "and it's a smart one, too," he added, taking the whole audience into his confidence, as he leaned forward across the counter. "Because a lot of things in this old world are passed off as gold when they are really only gold-*plated* — but now here's how you tell." And without taking it off her wrist, he pointed to something on the inner side of the bracelet.

"Now you see where it says 'fourteen K'? That means *'fourteen karat gold,'* and you see that little mark right there next to it? Well, that there is the government *stamp* and the mark-of-the-maker is what we call that, certifying that is *genuine gold.*" Like an expert lecturing on the subject, he indicated the marks to those, including Harold, who craned forward in avid interest — except for Lawrence, who continued to glare at the hoop-man — he who now assumed his most genial tone: "And I'll tell you what I'm gonna do, young lady, because my missus has gotten mighty fond of that bracelet, and her birthday is comin' up right soon, I am going to offer you" — and he pulled out a roll of bills from his pocket — "*fifty* dollars for that bracelet. Now it's your bracelet, no doubt about that, it is your property, won fair and square at a game of skill — so you're free to keep it, or" — he counted out five ten-dollar bills — "you're free to take the money — unless, of course, someone in the crowd would care to better the offer . . . though I can assure you it is a fair market price, maybe even a might on the high side because of my wife's birthday comin' up," adding this last with a neighborly chuckle.

"Take it," someone in the crowd prompted, "take the money."

"Hell yes," agreed another, "take the fifty."

The young woman looked at the faces in the crowd. And Harold realized she was looking at him.

"What would you do?" she asked with a gentle smile.

Harold was surprised. "Me?" He was also flustered. "Aw, I dunno — take the money, I guess."

She looked at the hoop-man. "I guess I *will* take the money," she said almost shyly — and she returned the bracelet and he handed her the money, which she carefully folded and put in her purse.

"All right!" said the hoop-man with sudden gusto, "there goes another big winner! And as long as we've got this roll of money out, let's just sweeten the pot!" So saying, he peeled off two fifties, rolled one up and tucked it in the band of the gold watch; the other he stuck inside the one already sticking out of the barrel of the pearl-handled .45.

"It's ten cents a hoop," he said, "it's six hoops for half a dollar. Everybody's a winner today!"

Harold was about to buy six more hoops, but Big Lawrence pulled on his arm. "Let's git outta here," he growled.

"What's the matter with you?" Harold wanted to know when they were clear of the crowd.

Lawrence was furious. "Don't you know that was pro'-bly his dang *wife?*" he demanded.

"Who?" asked Harold, looking back toward the hoop place. "You mean that woman that won the bracelet?"

"Yes!" Lawrence fairly shouted.

"His *wife?* What the heck would she be doin' there?"

Lawrence looked away in disgust, then spat. "Boy, are you *dumb!*"

"Well, I'll tell you one thing," said Harold stubbornly, "I'm gonna have a try at that six-gun before we leave here — *and* them fifties he stuck in the barrel!"

"They were in *cahoots*, dang it!"

"He give her the money, didn't he?"

"He give her the money 'cause I was 'bout to *ex*-pose him! That's why he give her the money! That son'bitch oughtta be strung up! An' I may be just the one to do it."

Lawrence continued ranting until they reached the Loop-O-Plane. Because of the outlandish nature of the ride — its obvious discomfiture and its apparent danger — there were more people watching it than waiting to ride it. A large sign read:

WARNING

DO NOT WEAR GLASSES, WRISTWATCHES,
JEWELRY, OR CARRY LOOSE CHANGE ON
THIS RIDE. THE MANAGEMENT IS NOT
RESPONSIBLE FOR THE SAFETY OF
PATRONS OF THE LOOP-O-PLANE.

"Let's ride it," said Lawrence gruffly, "unless they find out you're too dumb to trust on it."

"Will you shut up about that," said Harold impatiently. "You're just sore 'cause you didn't win nothin' at the hoop place."

"Dang, I can't even talk to you when you act so dumb. How much money you got anyway?"

"Five dollars."

"Is that all?"

"Why? How much have you got?"

"Seven-fifty . . . maybe more."

Harold took off his wristwatch and put it in his pocket as they approached the entrance. "Ain't you gonna take your watch off like the sign said?"

Lawrence scoffed. "Heck no, that's all bull."

The ride was a frightening one, spinning relentlessly, and turning them upside down with such violence that they reached out in reflexive desperation, their hands striking the top of the wire cage that kept them from falling out — the illusion of which was heightened by the straps across their laps being fairly loose, so that actually falling out of the contraption seemed imminent. It was during one of these reflexive hand-flings that Lawrence smashed his wristwatch against the top of the cage.

They emerged pale and shaken, but the shared experience seemed to have brought them closer.

"Dang," admitted Harold quietly, as they threaded their way through the curious onlookers, "I nearly peed in my pants on that last loop."

Lawrence flaunted his smashed watch as if it were a war trophy. "Look at that dang watch," he said. "Boy, it really took a lick to do that to it!"

"You reckon it's ruined?" asked Harold.

Lawrence frowned. "Aw, it wudn't worth a goddam anyway," he said. "I bought it fer a dollar off a ole nigger washerwoman." He raised his arm so that the crowd could see the broken watch, still on his wrist. "Don't wear your watch on the Loop-O-Plane!" he warned them, grinning crazily.

They walked along the midway, pausing at the roller coaster, which was called "The Killer," but Lawrence said the line was too long. "Let's go on the dang *wheel!*" he said, referring to the huge Ferris wheel, which was about three stories high. The seats on the Ferris wheel were simply short padded benches with a single bar across the front to hold the rider in. With some effort Lawrence got the bench seat rocking back and forth until it seemed like it was going to go all the way over. "Loop-O-Plane!" he kept yelling at the top of his voice. "This dang bar won't save us!" — and he would watch Harold's reaction. Harold knew the seat could not go all the way over, but then, when they were stopped at the very top and Lawrence was rocking the seat with all his might, causing them to be almost horizontal, he also began shaking the security bar and reaching under it, at the end where it was supposed to be locked in a complicated manner.

"I can unlock it!" he shrieked like someone possessed. "*I can unlock it!*" And he grappled at the locking mechanism in a pretense of frenzy, while still rocking them back and forth.

"*Kamikazi!*" he screamed. "*Kamikazi! Ai-eee!*"

"Are you crazy!" said Harold in real alarm now that it seemed the bar was about to unlock. Meanwhile, far below, the operator had his hands cupped and was yelling something up at them in what appeared to be urgent tones.

When they reached the bottom, the Ferris wheel operator, a burly westerner, stopped the wheel and made them get out.

"We ain't been round but once!" Lawrence objected.

"I seen what you was doin' up there," said the operator, his face flushed with anger. "You oughtta have your goddam head examined!"

Lawrence hitched up his pants and was ready to square off. "It was our money and our ride," he said. "I reckon we can do what we want on there."

"Not on my wheel you can't," said the other, as he put a teenage couple into the seat, secured the crossbar, and started up the wheel. "I see you 'round here again," he continued, raising a finger of caution, "I'll knock you to the goddam ground."

Harold started pulling Lawrence away. "Come on, dang it," he said.

"Whatta you mean 'again'?" Lawrence demanded of the operator. "I'm here right now, ain't I? Come on, you lard-ass, I'll tear your head off!"

From somewhere in the control box the operator withdrew a two-foot hardwood baseball bat — a souvenir from his distant past, inscribed "Louisville Slugger" — and looked directly at Harold. "You better git your friend outta here right quick, sonny, 'cause if I have to pull a 'Hey, Rube,' you boys will be in more trouble than you ever thought was possible. I mean, around here we can git down to the nut-cuttin' faster than you can *jack-off!*"

"Awright, we're goin'," said Harold, continuing to pull Lawrence by the arm, but now more forcefully. "Come on, dang it," he implored, "you're gonna get us throwed outta here — or worse."

While it was apparent that Lawrence did not like the idea of backing down, his resistance to being led away by Harold lessened noticeably after the appearance of the bat. "I'll stick that dang pecker-bat up his lard-ass A-hole!"

Lawrence warned, jerking his arm out of Harold's grasp, but moving along now, away from the wheel. "Did you see that lard-ass?" he went on. "Wouldn't stand up to me man to man! He had to pull a dang pecker-bat!"

"You could of got us killed," said Harold.

"Are you crazy? I could of took him apart!"

"I ain't talkin' 'bout him — I'm talkin' 'bout up on the wheel, the way you was swingin' the chair like a dang maniac."

"We done it before," said Lawrence, looking surprised. "We done it last year. Remember?"

"Yeah, but not like that," Harold insisted.

"Was you scared?" Lawrence wanted to know, leaning out to peer at him and grinning like a de-ment.

Now began another series of concession tents — these seemingly designed to catch the interest of the most sim-pleminded persons in attendance. The first was run by a man who sported a pencil mustache and a straw hat, both of the bygone style of the vaudeville stage. In each hand he held an ordinary rock, the size of a golf ball, and he would strike one against the other, punctuating his pitchman's pat-ter with the rifle-crack they made when he brought them together. Despite the rapid-fire delivery of his spiel, his face was without expression except for a quirky tic above the right corner of his mouth.

"Tell me something, boys" — his voice was a nasal singsong, speaking now directly to Harold and Lawrence as they approached — "when was the last time you had the extreme pleasure of breaking some of your momma's Sun-day dinner china? And didn't it feel mighty good to break those Sunday dinner-plates into about a thousand pieces?

You say you don't know the feeling because you've never dared to do it? Well, I'll tell you one thing, there aren't many feelings that I would rate higher on the pleasure scale — oh maybe one or two, depending on your age, if you get my meaning, hee-hee-hee." His laugh was grotesquely mechanical. "Yessir, I guess there's really nothing to compare with the thrill of smashin' those Sunday dinner-plates."

"What the heck's he talkin' about?" demanded Big Lawrence.

"Danged if I know," said Harold.

The pitchman was standing at a waist-high counter, and about twelve feet behind him was a structure just partly discernible because of a large cloth draped over it.

A small crowd had gathered, drawn by the indecipherable crack of the two rocks, and then held by the tic-face manner of the pitchman and the near hypnotic undulation of his patter.

"And now," he went on, "you too can experience that wonderful thrill," and he removed the cloth with a flourish. What was revealed looked like a big open china closet with dinner-plates on display, propped up vertically, facing the audience in rows of ten plates each.

Then, with considerable effort, the pitchman hefted a bushel basket to the counter — a basket filled with rocks like those he was holding.

"Two rocks for a nickel," he announced, "and five for a dime."

"Five!" said Lawrence, handing over a dime; he turned to Harold. "I always did wantta break some dang dinner-plates! Watch me go right down the whole line!"

He threw his first rock at the plate on the extreme left

of the top shelf. He threw it as hard as he could, and it was wide.

"Throw at one in the middle," advised Harold. "That way if you miss, you might hit one on either side of it."

"Are you crazy?" demanded Lawrence. "I'm goin' right down the line!" This time he threw with more control and shattered the plate he was aiming at. Although these "plates" were approximately the same size as ordinary dinnerware, they had been made of common red-dirt clay, indigenous to the region, and then dipped into a tub of whitewash. Lawrence proceeded to break three more in a row, but was dissatisfied with the dull crumpling sound they made when they broke.

"They ain't real plates," he complained to Harold, and then directly to the pitchman: "They're nothin' but ole Mex mud-plates!"

"Step aside, son," said the pitchman, softly but with ambiguous menace, "and give some of these other good folks a chance to play."

Several others were, indeed, trying to get to the basket of rocks, and Lawrence felt obliged to warn them. "They ain't real plates," he said again, but he was shouldered aside by a surge of farmhand types, mostly in their twenties, dressed in coveralls, their cheeks bulging with Red Man chaw.

Harold was also eager to get Lawrence moving. "Come on, dang it," he kept saying, as he pulled on Lawrence's arm, "let's find somethin' we can both do!"

Lawrence reluctantly let himself be towed along, but not without expressing his grievance: "I should've put my last rock right upside that A-hole's head!"

Not far beyond the rock-throw concession was another uniquely primitive enterprise: a metal pipe, forty feet high and four inches in diameter, had been sunk in the ground just deep enough to keep it from falling over, then covered from top to bottom with crankcase grease. At the bottom of the pole, and surrounding it, were boards forming a box that was filled with hay. Completing the curious rig was a tall wooden ladder, braced against the pipe. For a ten-cent admission a person could climb the ladder and slide down the greased pipe into the bed of hay. The price included the use of a pair of plastic overalls to keep the grease off.

"Try the Big Pole Slide!" the barker shouted. "Try the Big Pole Slide for only a dime!" From the ground it looked extremely high, and the ladder a perilous ascent.

Lawrence frowned when, after a minute of staring, he understood its nature. "Look at that," he said in disgust. "Only a moron would do anything that dumb!"

"What makes you say that?" asked Harold, but before Lawrence could attempt to explain, they were distracted by a puff of smoke overhead, accompanied by an unidentifiable noise — like the roar of a mechanical beast.

"Hey," said Lawrence, suddenly wild-eyed. "Hear that? That means they're openin' the dang *freak show!* Come on!"

They ran in the direction of the smoke cloud and the curious sound, toward the very end of the midway, where there was a large tent, emblazoned with colorful cloth carnival-tableaux, the kind that resembled, and in many cases actually were, huge oil paintings, most of them cracked and amber with age. Each was meant to represent something inside the tent — and while their artistic styles seemed to vary, all the renditions had one thing in common: a flair for the melodramatic.

In front of the tent was a raised stage on which one of the "show-people" would occasionally appear, as a partial inducement to draw in the crowd — a group of about ten or so by the time Harold and Lawrence arrived. The strange roaring sound had been shut off, the smoke had cleared, and the barker was in full cry: "*Adrian, the Great Hermaphrodite!*" he kept shouting, gesturing toward a robed and hulking sad-eyed personage seated on the stage. "Is it man, or is it woman? You say, 'Well, it is bound to be a man, because look at that beard!' But, of course, it *could* be a false beard — so I'm just going to ask someone from the audience, anyone at all, to step up and take a very close look at this so-called beard — how about you, son?" he said, fixing Harold with a stare. "You have the face of an honest boy, just climb on up here, please."

Harold was embarrassed, but Big Lawrence grinned crazily and said, "Go on, dang it," and practically hoisted Harold onto the stage.

"Now then, son," said the barker, "I want you to take a good close look at that beard! You touch it, you feel it, and you tell me and these people out here whether or not it's real!"

"Just don't pull it off!" taunted Lawrence from the crowd. "Haw!"

"No, you're wrong, son," said the barker to Lawrence. "He can pull it as much as he thinks necessary to prove that it's real — and I'll tell you one thing: some of it may come *out*, but it won't come *off*. And that's a fact."

The "Great Hermaphrodite" turned his or her face up

and to the side, so that Harold could examine the beard, which he did, aware mainly, however, of the heavy breathing of this very large person, and the strange, sad eyes, which Harold avoided looking into.

"It's all right," said the man/woman then in a voice so soft Harold could scarcely believe it came from this bearded hulk, "you can pull on it . . ."

But Harold could see that the beard was real — dark, thick, and curly like that of a Greek wrestler he had once seen.

"Yeah, it's real all right," he said, addressing his judgment to the barker, then to Lawrence and the others.

"Thank you, son," said the barker. "Now I want you to do just one more thing for me — I want you to take your hand, place it on the Great Herm's shoulder and pull down the robe."

"What?" said Harold, not understanding.

"Go ahead, son," said the barker, and the Great Herm took Harold's hand into his own, placed it on the shoulder of the robe, and gently pushed it down.

The crowd made a small but audible gasp and one or two nervous laughs as the robe was lowered to expose a large bare breast.

"I doubt that anyone will question the authenticity of the female bosom you now see before your eyes . . ."

Harold thought that it was probably a real breast all right; it was big enough, but he was not sure it was the right shape. He had seen Lawrence's sister's breasts when they had stood on an apple crate outside her bathroom window, when she would take a shower; and once, which was the most important time, when she came in after being parked in front of the house for a long time necking with a date, and when she got into the bathroom she had taken off her blouse and brassiere and stood in front of the mirror right under the light, massaging her breasts and watching in the mirror while she did it. Lawrence had been embarrassed. "What the heck is she doing?" he had demanded, and made an excuse for them to stop watching. "I heard a door open," he had said, which Harold knew wasn't true.

But the best, the most memorable time had been when his cousin, Caddy, who was a year older, had been visiting them, and one night they had gotten ready for bed and were having a snack in the kitchen, sitting at the table and he had gotten up to get the milk and then, in pouring some for her, had looked down at the glass, but had seen not so much the glass as the gap in her pajama top and the perfect pear of her bare breast, and — most striking of all it seemed — the pink nipple thrusting out, surprising him with its size and prominence, almost as though it were a separate part of her.

This was very different; the nipple of the Great Herm was practically unnoticeable — in fact, he realized, not unlike his own.

"Thank you, son," the barker said to him, "thank you for your assistance." And as Harold climbed down, he said in a spirited tone: "Proof positive of the combined male and female nature of the Great Hermaphrodite! And there is more! More proof positive of the sexual duality of the Great Hermaphrodite! On the inside! You will see both male and female reproductive organs of the Great Hermaphrodite! It's all on the inside!" He turned his attention to one of the illustrated banners and pointed with his cane. "See! On exhibit! Alice, the Alligator Girl!" The tableau showed a mermaid, with an alligator's tail and legs, and with wild blond hair and blazing eyes.

"And see!" He pointed to a tableau of a well-dressed man standing in front of a mirror, wearing a featureless leather mask. "On the inside! James Pomeroy! 'The Ugliest Man Alive'! James Pomeroy, whose face was so hideously disfigured in a train wreck seven years ago as to defy description! He has not yet undergone plastic surgery because of his pending lawsuit against the railway responsible for his monstrous appearance! So monstrous that he is compelled by law to wear a *mask* in public at all times! Ladies and gentlemen, inside the tent, *James Pomeroy will remove that mask!* And you will see the true horror of hideous facial disfiguration beyond your wildest dreams! And you will see Blue Thomas, the amazing six-legged mule from Missouri. Six legs, ladies and gentlemen, and a kick in every one of them! *And* on the inside! The original Colt forty-five pistol used by that notorious but beloved daughter of the Lone Star State, Bonnie Parker! A pistol with which she shot down seven lawmen in seven days! And you will see the world's most dangerous reptiles!" He raised his cane in a flourish, pointing it to one of the more flamboyant tableaux behind them; it featured an elephant encircled by a gigantic snake, the elephant's trunk upraised in a trumpeting cry of panic and rage. "The giant anaconda!" said the barker, "large enough to crush a full-grown elephant! You will see diamondback rattlesnakes, copperheads, cottonmouth water moccasins, the Gila monster, and the deadly Egyptian adder!" He paused and his cane adroitly touched the shoulder of the grave impassive person still seated on the stage, and his voice became solemn: "And on the inside, ladies and gentlemen, the Great Hermaphrodite will remove all of her garments, to reveal a complete duality of sex in every — I repeat, *every* — detail! Because while she is *all woman*, she is also *all man* . . . if you get my meaning. And last, but by no means least, you will meet, you will touch, you will play with . . . a walking, talking *aboriginal!* Yes, a true aboriginal from the deepest jungles of Western Borneo! I am referring now to Mister Dan, that funny little old monkey man! Is he human, or is he of the simian species? This is a question anthropologists the world over have not been able to agree on. Decide for yourself, after you've seen Mister Dan, that funny little old monkey man! All on the inside! Get your tickets here, twenty-five cents, the fourth part of a one-dollar bill, please don't crowd, folks . . ." As he took his place in the booth and started selling tickets, the machine producing the mechanical roar started up again.

"What's making that dang noise?" Lawrence asked as he gave the barker a quarter.

"All on the inside, sonny."

Inside, the tent was like a canvas hothouse — too small to accommodate the exhibits and the crowd of fifteen or twenty people who had filed in. Everyone was sweating profusely.

"Jesus H. Christ . . . ," complained Big Lawrence, wiping his brow, "it's hotter than a nun's poon in here! I can't take much of this . . ."

Most of the space was occupied by stuffed and bottled reptiles. In the center, however, against one wall of the tent, was a platform about three feet high, and on it, sitting in a folding chair, large and silent, was the Great Hermaphrodite. The barker mounted the two steps and stood alongside.

"Ladies and gentlemen, may I have your attention,

please. I am happy to present to you Madame X, the Great Hermaphrodite — that's right, I did say 'Madame,' because despite her hirsute" — and he smiled down at Harold and Lawrence, who appeared to be the youngest in the place, "— that means *hairy*, boys —" before continuing to the crowd: "yes, I say despite her hirsute characteristics, she is all woman. Madame X, will you please stand, and remove your robe?"

She slowly and gravely rose to her feet, removing the sash belt of her robe and pulling the edges aside for its entire length, revealing her large body, with two bare breasts, the left one — that which Harold had exposed — considerably larger than the other. Beneath the robe she wore a pair of olive-drab shorts, which covered her from her waist to midthigh.

"I now direct your attention," said the barker, "to the legs of Madame X," and as he spoke, she lifted one leg and stretched it to the side for all to see.

"They are hairless," he said, "as are her arms, and indeed, ninety-five percent of her entire body. Her bodily parts on which hair grows are her head, her face, and her pubic region — and, yes, under her arms. Would you lift your arms, please, Madame."

She did so, and great drops of sweat fell from her biceps to the platform floor. Her armpits, though without hair, were dark and appeared to have been dusted with white powder.

"You will notice," said the barker, "that Madame X has shaved beneath her arms — with typical feminine vanity."

This gave rise to a ripple of laughter from the crowd, including Lawrence, who added, with an elaborate grimace of distaste: "I sure wouldn't want my nose stuck up there! Haw!"

Harold edged away from Lawrence. He felt a vague sympathy for this strange bearded person, perhaps because he had shared the stage with her for a brief moment.

"Now then, let's get serious," said the barker. "I know what's in each and every one of your minds — you're asking yourself, 'Well, what about her genitalia — her private parts, her sexual parts — is it man, or is it woman?' Let me assure you that every person" — he paused and shot a straight look to Harold and Lawrence — "every *adult* person here today will have their curiosity satisfied — because, for one dime, less than the price of a postage stamp, we will accompany Madame X to her private quarters, where she will remove all of her garments and reveal her genitalia for all to see!"

"What the heck is that?" Harold wanted to know.

"That's her pecker an' poon," said Lawrence with a grin, then he scowled, "but he ain't gonna let us see it — 'cause *you* look too dang young!"

"Reckon I look as old as you do," said Harold. But the barker did not think either one of them looked old enough, so they were turned away from the inner sanctum of the Great Hermaphrodite.

Grossly incensed, Lawrence was prepared to storm out. "I bet she's got a dang false pecker anyway!" he said loud enough for everyone to hear.

The barker, with the Great Herm in tow, was leading the crowd through the opening to an adjoining tent. He gave Lawrence a humorless smile as they passed.

"Don't go diggin' no early grave for yourself, hoss," he said quietly.

Lawrence, now doubly incensed, stamped around the tent, which was now empty except for the taxidermy collection.

"We oughtta tear this place apart," he fumed.

Then he spotted a gap in the canvas wall of the tent, wrenched the frayed edges wider apart, and peered in.

"I'm gonna get a look at that dang pecker-poon yet," he muttered.

Harold had taken an interest in a preserved Gila monster and failed to notice Lawrence's tampering with the tent wall, until Lawrence suddenly turned toward him wild-eyed and grinning.

"Hey, c'mere," he whispered urgently, "it's the dang monkey man!"

"Huh?"

"The monkey man, the monkey man! It's him, dang it!" Lawrence moved his head so Harold could see, through the gap and into a small canvas cubicle. In the middle of the room was a metal bed, its raised sides fitted with vertical rungs, like a child's crib, and inside it sat a small, dark-skinned person with a tiny head, eating something held in both hands.

Harold nodded. "That's him all right."

"Hey, monkey man!" Lawrence hissed in a whisper. "Hey, Mister Dan!"

The small, bright-eyed aboriginal pulled himself up by the top rung of the crib and stared at the hole in the canvas.

"He heard you," whispered Harold. "He's lookin' right at us."

"Let's go in there an get 'im," said Big Lawrence.

"Are you crazy?"

"We can take him on the Loop-O-Plane," said Lawrence, grinning at Harold like a madman.

Harold stared at him "You must really be crazy," he said.

"You mean you're scared to go in there with me to get him?"

Harold gave him a look meant to reflect disgust. "What I mean," he said coldly, "is that they could get us for *kidnappin'*."

"He ain't no kid," said Lawrence, "he's a monkey man."

They crawled under the canvas wall, into the crib-tent, and crept up to the crib itself. Mister Dan offered no resistance when Lawrence picked him up, and, in fact, put his arms around Lawrence's neck.

"Look at this dang monkey man!" said Lawrence, pleased at the apparent show of affection. "Let's go get 'im some cotton candy and custard."

"It may make him throw up," said Harold.

They threaded the alleyway maze behind the tents of the oddities complex, Mister Dan now holding each of their hands, half running and half hopping between them. At the end of the passage between the tents, where it joined the midway, was another cotton-candy stand. While Harold and the aboriginal waited in the shadow of the tent, Lawrence ran over and came back with three cones of it. After a minute, Mister Dan had his wrapped around his head like a turban.

"How long you think it'll be before they start missin' him?" Harold wanted to know.

Lawrence shook his head. "Not long I reckon. Let's take him in yonder." He pointed to a sign over a barnlike building directly ahead of them:

Law West of the Pecos
Bar and Grill
THE BIGGEST BURGERS AND THE COLDEST BEER
AT THE ONION

The place was deserted except for a cowboy and two girls in a back booth. At the bar, Lawrence lifted Mister Dan onto a stool between them. He started spinning slowly around, pulling strands of the candy off his head and into his mouth.

"Three beers," said Big Lawrence and he slapped two quarters onto the bar.

The bartender was a man who should have worn glasses, but did not, so that his squinting had given his face in repose an expression of constant disapproval.

"You boys ain't old enough to drink beer," said the bartender.

"Okay," said Lawrence, "give us two *Cokes*, and give *him* a beer — *he's* old enough."

"That's right," said Harold, genial and positive, "he's supposed to be about fifty."

The bartender took two Cokes out of an ice chest, opened them, and sat them on the bar. "An' I don't serve niggers," he said.

"He ain't no nigger," said Lawrence, "he's a monkey man."

The bartender's frown deepened. "What?"

"It's true," said Harold, with what sounded like a touch of pride. "He works here at the Onion. They call him 'Mister Dan.' Ain't you heard that guy on the midway? He says, 'Come in an' see Mister Dan, that funny little old monkey man!' " He nodded at their companion. "Well, that's him."

"That'll be thirty cents," said the bartender, and he picked up the two quarters.

"Well, give 'im a beer," said Lawrence.

The bartender put two dimes back on the bar. "You boys drink up, an' haul ass," he said, "an' git him outta here."

"What're you gonna do," said Lawrence, "pull a dang 'Hey Rube' on us? Haw."

From the back booth the cowboy's drunken but friendly voice was heard: "Hey there, hoss, how 'bout two beers for two dears back here? An' bring me a Coke setup."

While the bartender was taking the two beers and the Coke setup to the booth in the back, Lawrence surreptitiously removed a half-pint of Wild Turkey from his pocket and poured some into his and Harold's Coke bottles.

"Try an' give 'im some Turkey," he told Harold.

Harold looked at their companion, who was slowly spinning on the barstool, while pulling the cotton candy out in long strands and draping them sideways across his face, all in a slightly wild-eyed, but nonmenacing, fashion. But before Harold could get his attention, the bartender had returned, looking serious.

"I seen you just now, toppin' them Cokes with Turkey," he said. "I want you to pick up your change an' haul ass."

Lawrence cleared his throat.

"This here's a public place," he said with considerable authority. "I reckon we can stay here as long as we want." He looked to Harold for affirmation.

125

"That's right," said Harold, nodding, "it's a public place."

"Public place hell," said the bartender. "I *own* this bar, it's private property."

"This ain't no real bar," said Lawrence, "this here's a *concession* — you don't own it, you jest *rent* it." He indicated Mister Dan with a jerk of his head. "So why don't you give him a beer before we tangle ass-holes."

It was then they noticed that the bartender was squinting beyond them, through the open door, across the dirt street, where, next to the cotton-candy concession, stood a tall man in khaki, wearing a Stetson on his head and a pearl-handled .45 on his hip.

"You jest wait here, son," said the bartender. "I'm gonna git that deputy to put you . . . an' him . . . an' your nigger frien' . . . *under* the goddam jail."

"You ain't man enough to tangle," Lawrence yelled after him.

"Hey, we better get outta here," said Harold, watching as the bartender started across the dirt street toward the deputy.

"Yeah . . . ," Lawrence was reluctant to admit, "I recktum."

Now the bartender was talking to the deputy and pointing toward the bar. "Come on, let's head out the back."

"What about Mister Dan?" asked Harold.

Now the bartender and the deputy were coming toward them. Lawrence scooped up the monkey man. "Awright, let's head out!" he exclaimed, obviously with a full head of adrenaline now in anticipation of the chase.

They hurried toward the back, passing the booth where the cowboy and the two girls were partying.

"Hey, where you good-lookin' boys goin?" one of the girls yelled.

The cowboy laughed. "Looks like they're headed fer tall cotton," he said.

"What's that big un' carryin'?" one of the girls wanted to know. "Looked like a old niggerman."

"That wudn't no nigger," said the cowboy.

"He was carryin' him jest like a li'l baby," she said. "Jest like a li'l babe-in-arms!"

"I think you're drunk, hon," said the cowboy. "Here, have another one."

In the dark corridor leading past the deserted kitchen and to the back door, they passed several coat hooks on the wall, one of which had an old jacket hanging on it.

"Git that dang coat," said Lawrence.

"You mean steal it?" asked Harold.

"No, jest git it!"

Before they reached the back door, Lawrence took the jacket and draped it over the monkey man's head and shoulders.

"Awright now," Lawrence said as they stepped out into the blazing reality of the Texas afternoon, "try an' ack natch'ral."

They headed for the less frequented area of the livestock and produce exhibitions.

"What's he doin' in there?" Harold wanted to know after a few minutes.

Lawrence lifted the top of the jacket and peered in.

"Jest settin' there," he said. "Hey, did you see them two girls in the booth back yonder? They were ready to have a party."

"Looked like they *were* havin' a party," said Harold.

"I don't think they liked that shit-kicker they was with," said Lawrence. "They were mighty friendly. I got half a mind to git rid of this monkey man an' head back there. Think we oughtta?"

"Are you crazy?" asked Harold. "He's awready called the law on us." He looked at the bundle in Lawrence's arms. "Besides," he went on, "we can't jest up an' leave him, can we?"

"Awright then," said Lawrence. "You carry him."

Harold was reluctant.

"We better not switch, he's probly got use' to you by now."

Lawrence seemed pleased by this notion, but was not prepared to admit it.

"Hell, he wudn't even notice," he said, but he lifted the jacket for a glimpse. The monkey man stared at him with wide unblinking eyes and an expression of mild concern. Then he slowly opened his mouth, at the same time screwing up his face in an extremely curious, but unthreatening, grimace.

"Just look at this dang monkey man!" exclaimed Lawrence, and he laughed aloud. "Ain't he somethin'!" He gave the bundle an affectionate squeeze. "I'm gonna run with 'im," he said, "an' see what he does!"

And he took off in a sprint, along the thoroughfare between the livestock and the produce exhibitions, where only a few people were strolling, most of them elderly couples. Lawrence ran past them, yelling in a loud voice: "Look out! I got the monkey man! Coming through with Mister Dan, that funny little ole monkey man!"

The monkey man, now half uncovered, had gotten quite

excited by the rushing about, and began to make high-pitched squealing sounds of apparent delight, waving his arms, gesticulating wildly, and grimacing in an extraordinary way.

Heads turned at the curious sounds and the spectacle.

"Did you see that? Did you see that boy runnin' like a crazy person an' carryin' a little niggerman? Good Lord!"

"Oh no, I don't think it was a nigger. It didn't look like no nigger to me."

"Well what the hell was it?"

"Sounded to me like he said 'the monkey man.' "

"*Whut?*"

Harold had to run full out to catch up with them.

"Be careful!" he yelled at Lawrence. "Don't drop him. Don't drop Mister Dan!"

The notion somehow tickled Lawrence.

"Don't drop the monkey man!" he yelled at the top of his voice, and he lifted him to his shoulder for all to see. Mister Dan was squealing and grimacing in a sort of joyous consternation.

Here the thoroughfare crossed the midway, and someone from one of the shows must have recognized him, because the "Hey Rube!" cry went up, and two men in coveralls converged on Harold and Lawrence, yelling:

"Hey Rube! They've got Mister Dan! Hey Rube!"

"We gotta start lookin' for tall cotton," said Lawrence as he took Mister Dan from his shoulder and lowered him to the ground.

"Good-bye, monkey man!" he said, pulling Harold by the arm. "Let's head for the dang pickup!"

So they took off, leaving the monkey man with the jacket

still draped around him. One of the two men picked him up, while the other one chased after Harold and Lawrence — past the rock-throwing concession, behind the Loop-O-Plane, and almost to the big Ferris wheel itself, before he realized they were long gone.

XII

BIG NAIL sat near the back of the half-empty Greyhound, next to a window so encrusted with red dust that it was barely translucent, despite the blazing afternoon sun that seared the bone-dry countryside.

After he had left the farmhouse, he had gone to the toolshed, located a chisel and a heavy hammer, and removed his leg-iron. So that, wearing ordinary work clothes instead of his prison garb, and without the telltale leg-iron, he appeared quite normal — except for his scarred and deadly countenance. He gazed dully out the window, seeing almost nothing because of the dust-caked glass; but, as the bus slowed to a stop in front of the war monument in the main square of a dusty little town, Big Nail was able to make out clearly three of the very few words he knew — not because he could read them, but like Pavlov's dog, he had learned to recognize them, now emblazoned across a big gold star on the side of a glistening white automobile: TEXAS STATE POLICE. The furrows of his brow narrowed to an even darker interest.

"Sweet fuckin' Jesus," he muttered, "don't leave me now."

A part of his mind leaped back to the ditch and the voices yelling behind him. "Git 'im!" he heard Cap'n say again. "Git that black son'bitch! Blow 'im in two!"

And then his brain was flooded with the image of a bull-mastiff that Cap'n had been training to fight in the pit, the dog laboring on a crude treadmill, with two weights hooked to its lower jaw, the gaping mouth dripping blood and saliva.

"The heavier the weight," Cap'n had said, "the sharper the bite."

And Bull Watson had snickered and spat a trail of Red Man across the room, before he replied: "Wal ah *reck-tum*."

The image had returned to Big Nail in a dream; except in the dream *he* was the dog, and it wasn't Cap'n and Bull Watson in the dream, it was always somebody else.

Now the police car, which seemed to have been lazily browsing at the corner near the bus stop, slowly nosed up and, with just enough screech of rubber to suggest potential drama, peeled away from the curb and headed down the highway out of town. Big Nail sighed heavily.

"Sweet mutha-fuckah," he said half aloud. "Gimme a sharp bite today!"

If his countenance and the subdued rage there softened for a moment when the police car left, it clouded again as he looked up, into the face of a white boy of about seventeen — a boy who, as the bus pulled away from its stop, had left his seat to walk down the aisle, hesitant and nervous, but finally managing to lean over and say in a genial tone: "Excuse me . . . I'm a student at Arlington College . . . and we're doing a study on low-rent housing in this area of Johnson County, and I was wondering if I could ask you a few questions . . ."

Big Nail glowered. "Say *whut?*"

The young man tentatively eased himself down on the armrest of the seat and repeated his question.

"What we're interested in," he went on, "is the low-rent housing situation in this county."

Big Nail did not reply at once, but gazed at the large many-dialed wristwatch that had been exposed on the young man's arm when he moved to sit down, bracing himself with one hand against the back of the seat in front of them, and continuing to talk as though now having committed himself too far to turn back.

"Would it be okay to, uh, ask you a few questions about the housing situation in your area?"

"Uh-huh." Big Nail raised his dull killer-gaze to the young man's blue eyes. "What's you want to know 'bout dat, uh, 'situation'?"

The young man asked the questions he had on a printed sheet, jotting down the answers in a small notebook. After a few queries, however, it became apparent that Big Nail's situation was somewhat atypical, and perhaps of dubious value for a survey of this nature.

"Ah been away from this place," Big Nail explained. "Ah been gone on a *trip*, you see what ah mean."

The student was understanding and very polite. He did not know if Big Nail was telling the truth about having been on a trip or simply did not wish to respond to personal questions. In either case, he was prepared to forego the questionnaire in favor of general conversation, which was not long in occurring.

"Lemme ast you somethin'," said Big Nail after a minute. "How much do a watch like that cost?"

The student was not sure about the price of the watch, but at least it was a talking point, and he made the most of it. Indeed he was so loquacious that Big Nail felt obliged to interrupt at one point, laying a hand on the young man's arm.

"Would you, uh, *read* somethin' for me?" he asked, and he took a small folded square of lined tablet paper from his shirt pocket. It was limp and soiled from age and handling.

"Ah think ah know what it say," he continued, handing over the paper, "but I want to be sure that I do, if you know what ah mean."

The young man seemed pleased by the opportunity to help someone in the other's circumstances.

"Certainly," he said, unfolding the paper, "I'd be more than glad to."

He looked at the smudged and creased page from the dimestore lined writing tablet, and it was apparent from his slight frown of distance and consternation that he had never before encountered, nor perhaps imagined, so primitive a document. The words had been printed in an unsure and tentative manner by a thick leaded pencil and were spelled phonetically:

THE WELFAIR TOLE ME TO RITE YOU
BECUSE OF BOOKER AND THE LAW
THAT SAY I HAB TO TRY TO *CONTACK*
YOU TO GIT THE WELFAIR FOR
BOOKER. C.K. HAS TRY TO HELP. HE IS
GOOD TO BOOKER. I HAB TO GO TO
WORK NOW. TRY AND DONT HURT
NOBODY ELSE.   CORA LEE

Somewhat self-consciously, but without much difficulty otherwise, the young man read the letter aloud to Big Nail, then refolded it and handed it back to him.

Big Nail grunted and muttered, "That what ah thought it say," as he accepted the letter and replaced it in his pocket, adding, "Ah obliged."

"You're very welcome," said the young man, perhaps not really having understood the other's remark.

XIII

THAT EVENING at supper Harold's mother announced that they would be receiving a visit from Aunt Flora and Caddy — her sister and her sister's thirteen-year-old daughter.

"They're driving down to Mexico City," she said, "and they'll stop over and spend the night, and start out again the next day. It'll be a nice way for them to break their trip, won't it?"

They were city folks, with different, perhaps higher, values and very sensitive in many and unusual ways — all of which Harold's mother felt she could, if not fully understand, at least appreciate; she was anxious that nothing upset them.

"We have to decide," she said, "which one of those horses would be best for Caddy."

Harold scoffed. "She can't ride worth a lick anyway." He looked at his father to confirm it, but his mother went on: "No, Flora said she's been taking lessons and that she goes riding in the park every Saturday morning."

It did not sound right to Harold, and he made a face. "In the dang park . . . ," he muttered.

"Now you can just stop it," said his mother firmly. "Caddy is your first cousin and she's a wonderful girl. So stop being so silly."

Harold's grandfather looked up from his plate.

"Is that Flo's girl you're talking about?" he asked. "Caddy? Is that who you're talking about?"

"Why yes it is, Granddad," said Harold's mother, pleased at his show of interest. "You remember Caddy, don't you? She visited us last year."

"Hell yes, I remember her," he said. "An' I'll tell you something else too — that little girl has the makings of a blue-ribbon *rump* on her, an' that's a fack!"

Harold's mother made a face and shook her head.

"Granddad," she demanded, "what on earth are you talking about?" She glanced uneasily at Harold and his father.

"Well, I'm tryin' to tell you," the old man went on, "them jeans she was wearin' looked like they was a couple of ripe mushmelons back there. I've never seen better," he declared, then added, "on any gal her age."

"Granddad . . . ," pleaded Harold's mother. "You get sillier every day."

But he was adamant. "She's a dead ringer for her mother at that age," he said. "Or that part of her is anyway. Don't you remember what a cutter Flo use' to be? Why she could sashay with the best of 'em!"

Harold's mother was exasperated. "Granddad . . . ," she said, drawing out the word. "Flo is still a young, beautiful woman. You talk about her like she was some kind of old maid. Good heavens."

"Of course she's a beauty," said the old man, "an' so was *her* mother — so you shouldn't be surprised that Caddy is developin' the way she is."

"Well I wouldn't trust her to ride Blackie," said Harold.

"Of course not," said his mother, glad that the subject was changing. "He's too wild and crazy for her."

"He ain't wild," said Harold with as much emphasis as he dared, "an' he sure ain't crazy neither."

"Don't say 'ain't,' Son," his mother said.

"He's just high-spirited, hon," said Harold's father. "I reckon that's what you mean."

"He's got a cockeye," she said. "I noticed it again the other day."

"Just a mite high-spirited," repeated his father, as if that settled it, but he went on: "I reckon we could borrow that horse of Les Newgate's again."

His mother brightened. "Yes, that's the one she rode last time, isn't it?"

Harold sighed. "If you want to call it that," he said.

"That roan-colored horse of Les Newgate's," his mother went on. "Yes, that's a very nice horse." She looked at Harold. "Would you ask him, Son?"

"Yes ma'm," Harold said, as stiff and formal as he could manage.

"And stop being so silly," his mother added.

When Aunt Flora and Caddy came for a visit down from Dallas, they often brought small expensive gifts from Neiman Marcus — scarves, gloves, neckties, billfolds, and the like for Harold and the two men, and a cashmere sweater for Harold's mother and occasionally a piece of exotic lingerie. This time they brought hunting vests for Harold and his father — quite fancy, with ammo pockets of soft leather — a pair of small German binoculars for his grandfather, and a lacy camisole for his mother.

"Caddy picked it herself," said Aunt Flo.

"It's lovely, hon," said his mother to Caddy, and kissed her.

Caddy had recently become a cheerleader at her high school, and had worn her purple sweater and white pleated skirt for them to see. She was blond and blue-eyed and as cute as a girl of thirteen could be. Harold's mother asked her to show them one of the routines she was learning, so she did a few cheerleading jumps and turns on the front porch. It was also the first time that her mother had seen her perform.

"Caddy," said Aunt Flo at one point, "try not to let your skirt go so high when you twirl like that."

"*Mo-ther* . . . ," said the girl in exasperation, "that's the way it's supposed to go! Good grief!"

On this visit, in addition to the gifts and the cheerleading demonstration, Aunt Flo and Caddy had brought with them their dedication to Moon, a new card game that was all the craze in the cities and towns of Texas at the time, and Harold and his mother were obliged to play the game with them. So now, after supper, when the dishes had been cleared away, and Harold's father and grandfather had gone into the parlor, where the bookcase of *National Geographics* was kept, and had settled down to reading the local papers or listening to the radio, Harold was required to forgo his game of catch or fungo practice with C.K. and sit down with his mother and Aunt Flora and Caddy at the round kitchen table for a game of Moon.

It was not a complicated game, but a certain amount of scorekeeping was required on the part of the person designated to do so. It seemed quite natural that Caddy, as the genuine aficionado of the game, should be the first to keep score, and Harold had provided her with the paper and pencil to do so. After half a dozen hands, however, she made her mouth into a petulant rose and said, "I just wish somebody else would keep score for a while."

"Why don't you try it, Son," his mother said.

And when Harold agreed, Caddy brought the paper and pencil around to his side of the table. She showed Harold the figures on the paper and explained what they meant. At first she was just standing next to him, but her arm was so close to his that he was certain he could feel the body heat of it. He was wondering if she would lean forward or kneel down to better explain, which she did, in an even more perfect way than he had conceived, resting a bare golden arm on the table, and leaning her head forward so that one or two blond locks dangled indolently just above the paper. The whole thing, beginning with her getting up from her chair on the opposite side of the table — the languid poise of her perfect cheerleading body rising from her chair, her hands for an instant smoothing the front of her skirt as in, or so it seemed, an involuntary caress — then the fluid movement around the table, and finally, and for some reason the most extraordinary thing of all: the incredibly sweet scent that preceded — like the heralding of something angelic — the fall of her hair past his face as she lowered her head.

"Sorry about my unruly mop," she said, as the golden strands momentarily touched the paper.

"That's okay," Harold managed, and she gave him an American cherry-pie girl-next-door smile that was dazzling.

Now, as she leaned over the table, the upper part of her arm pressing his, her face only inches away, the slender gold chain-locket dangling in what seemed to be a free and careless manner, Harold knew that if she were wearing anything other than her cheerleader sweater, he would, at this angle, be looking down at her breasts, as he had last year with the gaping pajama top. He tried to recall exactly how they looked, to fit the remembered image with the pert mounds confronting him now from beneath her sweater, which was neither tight nor loose but just right so that they might have appeared like nesting birds, soft and warm, even occasionally stirring, or so it seemed.

The first time the pencil fell to the floor was a complete accident. Harold, somewhat unnerved after his moment of scorekeeping instruction, had replaced the pencil on the table by the paper in so careless a way that it simply rolled off and fell to the floor. He felt it strike the top of his foot and fall forward, toward the center of the table. Although he was embarrassed about the awkwardness of having dropped it, he was relieved that before leaning down to re-trieve it, he was certain he knew exactly where it would be, so that the incident would not be prolonged by his having to grope about looking for it. And indeed it was there, when he leaned over, just as he had imagined, on the floor in front of his left foot. What he was not prepared for, however, was the extraordinary spectacle presented by the rest of the scene. He did not notice, at least for very long, what was happening with the legs and feet of his mother and Aunt Flora, for his gaze, as if it were a heat-seeking missile, went straight to Caddy. Her feet, in brown-and-white saddle shoes and short white socks, were quite properly close together; but her knees were about as wide apart as her skirt would allow them to be. Harold was so astonished that for the moment he was unable to register the visual image, only the realization that it was there. Then he picked up the pencil and this time allowed his eye to focus — on the left bare dimpled knee, then quickly along the golden curving thigh to the magical white V, which seemed to Harold to represent the ultimate achievement of the experience.

As he raised himself and replaced the pencil by the paper, he avoided at all costs looking at anyone, even wondering if they somehow knew. He felt that having done it was wrong, but it was too extraordinary a thing to regret. He felt it was somehow much more serious than what he and Lawrence had experienced at his sister's bathroom window. And he knew Lawrence would envy him for it. But he also knew he did not intend to share it.

After that, Harold played the game quietly and intently, as he tried to muster up the courage to do it again; but with no success. Then it was his turn to deal the cards; he was shuffling them and, without his having even considered such a possibility, a card flipped out during the shuffle and fell in his lap, and then, still without connivance, as if to crown the festival of serendipity, the card fell to the floor. On this occasion, when Harold retrieved the card he was prepared, and he believed or imagined that by now his eyes were more accustomed to the half-light beneath the table — where, as he soon discovered, the fabulous tableau remained unchanged, but was even enhanced when, during the fleeting eternity while his eyes devoured the sublime spectacle, one of Caddy's hands resting on her right leg just above the knee, began absently, carelessly to rub a small area of her leg, just above the knee. Despite better judgment, Harold risked another instant so that his gaze could retravel the enchanted stretch from knee to the mysterious sheen of the white triangle there, even allowing himself the luxury of a split millisecond of speculation as to the color of the hair behind it.

Following this triumph, he felt sated and was determined not to press his luck — that is, until Caddy, reacting to some development in the game, or perhaps for no reason at all, shifted in her chair. Harold immediately wondered if her movement had caused a change in the undertable tableau and, in the end, he could not resist one last artful drop of the pencil — and an extraordinary thing occurred: the young girl had indeed changed her position; her legs were now together — closely, securely, together. Harold felt strangely relieved, as if something that had gotten dangerously out of hand was back to normal. He quickly retrieved the pencil, glad that it was all over and feeling only a slight guilt about his behavior. But in the instant he began raising himself, and his eyes, the legs miraculously parted, affording one last riveting glimpse. But what was to become the most haunting and consuming thing of all was his gradual speculation as to whether or not she had deliberately parted them, aware all along of his craven antics.

The cotton harvest began the day Aunt Flo and Caddy arrived. Harold might have joined C.K., Lawrence, and a few others to go over to Farney and make some extra money picking cotton at the big syndicate farm; but because of their visitors, his mother had asked him to stay home and go horseback riding with Caddy.

Harold had imagined that Caddy would appear in some kind of strange foreign-outfit, and he was relieved when she turned up in ordinary faded jeans and what looked like a boy's shirt.

He was also greatly relieved, and even pleased, when it became apparent that she had become a much better rider since the last time, because he knew he would be blamed if she fell off the horse or had a similar mishap.

She was riding the horse he had borrowed from Les Newgate — a roan mare not much more spirited than an ordinary farm horse, ideal for the walking gait with which they set off for the pond, Harold making a mental note to avoid the pasture where the red bull stayed, and hoping that he had not somehow gotten out. Most of his thoughts, however, dwelt on the events of the previous evening. He did not recall having ever behaved in such an underhanded and incomprehensible manner. The earlier business of spying on Lawrence's sister through the bathroom window was done, he felt, simply because they knew it was wrong, and somewhat dangerous; and also it had been Lawrence's idea. But there had not been the compulsion, the crazed urgency he had felt last night in retrieving the pencil.

He could still not entertain the notion that she might have been aware of what he was doing; it was too fantastic. Surely she would have kicked over the table, exposing him, denouncing him, and storming out of the house, leaving his mother and Aunt Flora sobbing hysterically, and his father reaching for an ax handle, if not the ax itself. And so of course the parting of her legs during the last time had been a total coincidence — just an absent, reflexive, involuntary movement; he would have to be crazy to imagine anything else.

The presents from Neiman Marcus that Caddy and her mother usually brought with them were always extraordinarily packaged — beautiful and glittering gift-wrapping being one of the store's most exclusive hallmarks. Harold never failed to be impressed by the extravagant beauty of the wrapping — and then, of course, equally impressed to see that the quality of the gift seemed, after all, to warrant such finery of presentation.

Now in a flash of recollection, Caddy's legs beneath the table, close together prim and proper, the bare dimpled knees then slowly parting, and the golden limbs, finally to reveal at their apex the triangle of white panty sheen. Wasn't this perhaps the most elaborate, and appropriate of all gift wrappings? And if so, was it being offered as such?

"Are you always this quiet?" Caddy wanted to know, having to lean out from her saddle to get his attention.

"Huh?"

"What were you thinking about just now?" she pressed on.

"Oh, you mean just now?" said Harold, having to come out of it, somewhat more abruptly than he might have liked.

"Nothing really I guess."

Just as they arrived at the pond, it began to rain. They stopped under a large willow and tethered the horses. Caddy secured her reins by knotting them around the nearest limb, but when she saw Harold do a one-hand corral cinch, she was intrigued.

"How on earth did you do that?" she asked, her eyes wide and very blue.

So Harold was obliged to show her the simple manip-
ulation of the two leather straps, having to hold her hand
and guide it through the move. In doing it he had to stand
on her right-hand side, very close and slightly behind her.
He was careful not to press against her, but even so the
pressure was there — between their upper arms — and un-
expectedly, but most notably, between Harold's upper leg
and Caddy's right hip. And he was again aware of the extraordinary fragrance of her hair, now only inches from his
cheek. As he looked down to where his hand was holding
and guiding hers, he was looking past the open collar of the
shirt she was wearing — a boy's cotton shirt, with the top
three buttons undone — looking past it, but perhaps not
entirely past it, because what also registered in his periph-
eral vision was the gold locket, resting at the end of its slender chain, between her two perfect breasts, each of which
were gift-wrapped, as it were, in a floral filigree edged with
lace.

"Neiman's," she said, catching his eye while it lingered.
"Like it?"

Before Harold could consider a response, she took his
arm. "Look, there's a dry spot," she said, indicating the
ground next to the trunk of the tree where the overhanging
boughs were most dense.

"It's a set," she went on while Harold was sitting down
with his back against the tree, and when he looked up she
undid the first button on her beltless jeans.

"See?" she asked brightly, opening them just enough to
reveal the top two or three inches of her matching panties
— all done with such apparent ingenuousness that Harold
could only marvel at how oblivious she seemed to the effect
she could have on other people.

"Well?" she asked as she buttoned her jeans and sat down opposite him.

"What?"

"Did you *like* them?" she wanted to know, laughing and flipping a twig at him to show her impatience.

"Oh, sure," he said in a somewhat perfunctory manner, then added in a voice that trailed away: "They're . . . wonderful." He could not recall ever having used the word before.

The rain had gradually softened and finally stopped altogether, so that now, on the bank of the pond, under the great green canopy of the willow, it was like an oasis. Caddy stretched herself, one limb at a time, like a cat.

"This is marvelous," she said. "Do you spend a lot of time here?"

Harold felt overcome with awkwardness. "You mean here, under the tree?"

Caddy laughed, then looked serious. "I want to ask you something," she said, "and I promise I won't be mad if it's true." She looked at him expectantly.

"What do you mean?" asked Harold, feeling panicky.

She smiled. "Were you looking up my skirt last night?"

"When?" he demanded, looking hurt and confused.

Caddy laughed. "When you kept picking things up under the table."

Harold felt his face grow hot with the flush of doom; he couldn't meet her blue eyes, which now were dancing with mischief.

"I told you I wouldn't be mad," she reminded him.

But it was no good; how could he possibly believe her? It had to be a trick to make him confess to his outrageous behavior. He could only sit there immobilized with guilt and some nameless apprehension. Caddy stood, stretching her arms again, her body in silhouette for a moment, and Harold saw, as if for the first time, what was involved in the pressure he had felt on his upper leg when demonstrating the corral cinch — namely, her teenage cheerleader's blue-ribbon rump, boyishly narrow, but with softly rounded cheeks, looking pert and perfect in her snug-fitting jeans. She sighed, smiled, moved to where he was sitting and knelt down beside him. Despite his state of flushed and numbed immobility, he was immediately struck by the now most familiar fragrance of her hair, and he vaguely wondered if she had somehow managed to put more on in the last few minutes.

"Tell me what you saw," said Caddy.

"How do you mean?" asked Harold, hoping for a great deal more time.

Caddy sighed again. "Well, when you were looking up my skirt, what did you see?"

"Well you know," said Harold trying somehow to deprecate its significance, "your legs and so on."

"So?" Caddy wanted to know.

"What?"

"And so what did you *think?*" She pursued it, relentlessly. "What did you think about what you saw?"

"Aw, I dunno," said Harold.

Caddy laughed aloud.

"I really do like you, Harold," she said. "I like you a whole lot."

And she leaned out and kissed him, quite firmly, on the cheek.

When Harold didn't react right away, she gave him a searching look, and crinkled her nose.

"And now what are you thinking?"

He had to clear his throat.

"Well, that it's too bad," he managed, "that you're just passin' through."

"Oh, I'll be back," said Caddy, and showed him a sparkling smile. "I'll be back before you even know it! Come on, I'll race you to the house!"

And he could only watch as she skipped over to her horse, and away.

XIV

THE THREE MILES of dirt road that connected the farm to the highway was, depending on the weather, a near impassable quagmire or a clay-hard stretch of axle-breaking ruts. When Harold and C.K. went into town in the pickup, Harold usually drove the dirt stretch, but then, at the highway, would let C.K. take over, because of being underage himself. Lately, however, Harold's father had said that C.K. should drive the dirt stretch as well — "so he can get the practice in" — which he did, with great caution, never wanting to be in the position of having to explain some crippling mishap that befell the all-important pickup truck while he was at the wheel. Harold was slightly the better driver of the two, having had more experience, and was ever impatient with C.K.'s prudence.

"Dang it, C.K.," he whined now, as they crept along in second gear, a plaintive western tune droning over the dashboard radio. "I never seen nobody drive so all-fired dumb in my life. You drive jest like a ole nigger washerwoman!"

But C.K. was not impressed. "Uh-huh, you jest egg me

on, that's what you do — you jest hope ah bust axle on this stretch — then you git to drive it . . . ah know what you do. So you see, maybe ah ain't so dumb as you think ah is. Hee-hee."

Harold's impatience turned to annoyance. "Are you crazy? You really think I want us to bust the axle? All you got to do is drive *'tween* the ruts — you ain't gonna bust no axle."

"Well, when ah finish study this stretch a few more time, ah do that, ah drive it like you, 'tween the rut — right now ah gonna take it easy, ah don't hit no big rock neither." He reached over and turned the dial on the radio.

"Hey," said Harold, "that's good music." He started twisting it back the other way.

C.K. grimaced in disgust. "That ole ricky-tick? That ain't even worth listen to. Ole ricky-tick like that."

"Are you crazy? That's Ernest Tubbs!"

C.K. snorted. "Ole tub o' lard, that's who that is."

"Dang, C.K., when it comes to music, you are as dumb as they git." He found the station again. "Now listen to that — that's good music."

C.K. shook his head firmly. "Ah ain't listen to no ole ricky-tick!" His face contorted in exaggerated pain. "Ah wish ah had somethin' ah stick in my ear. How come you goin' in town anyway? Ah thought Big Lawrence an' you frien' Tommy done gone to the summer camp."

Harold looked out the window. "Well, I'm goin' in to help you load them sacks of feed, what'd you think I was goin' in for?"

"Oh, ah know why you goin' in, you don't shuck me none, you goin' in 'cause you don't want to hep you momma churn no butter, that's why you goin' in, hee-hee."

*   *   *

C.K. had started their practice of stopping at certain places in town by saying he "had some business to take care of."

Harold had snorted. "Sure," he said, "you gotta pick up eight sacks of feed an' two rolls of bob-wire — that's the business you got to take care of."

C.K. had frowned, shaking his head. "Ah ain't talk 'bout that business. Ah ain't study that business right now. Ah talk 'bout some personal business ah got to tend to. You unnerstan' what ah say?"

"Uh-huh, well I'll tell you one thing," Harold had said. "We ain't gonna take all day doin' whatever it is you do down in there."

C.K. had smiled. "Ah nevah said we was, did ah?"

And this had involved their crossing into a section that was known on maps, town records, and the like as "West Central Tracks" but was, in fact, spoken of simply as "Nigger Town" — and then, driving through the outlandishly bumpy labyrinth of dust, and lean-to shacks, beside which great black-charred iron washpots steamed in the Texas sun above raging bramble-fires, and black people sat or squatted in front of these ramshackle front porches, making slow cabalistic marks in the dust with a stick, or gazing trancelike at the road in front of them — driving through, and finally pulling in with the pickup, into the dirt front yard of one of the shacks.

Then at last they would be in the dark interior itself — seemingly windowless, smelling of kerosene and liniment, red beans and rice, cornbread, catfish, and possum stew — and Harold would sit in the corner with a glass of water given him and maybe a piece of hot cornbread, while C.K. sat at the table, in the yellow glow of the oil lamp, eating, always eating, forever dipping the cornbread into a bowl, head lowered in serious eating, but laughing too, and above all, saying things to make the big woman laugh, she who stood, or sat, watching him eat, his aunt, cousin, girlfriend, Harold never knew which, nor cared, until the talk about Cora Lee began. And afterward, on the way out of the section, they would stop again, at the Paradise Bar, so that C.K. could "see a friend," while Harold, saying, "Goddang it, C.K., we can't fool around here all day," waited in the pickup, drinking a Dr Pepper and eating a piece of hot barbecued chicken or spareribs that C.K. had brought out to him. But finally he had started going inside, tentatively at first, either to get C.K. out of there, or to get another Dr Pepper for himself, only then perhaps to linger in watching the crap-game awhile, or listening to Blind Tom sing the blues — so that in the end all pretense of "calling on C.K.'s people" had been discarded, and whenever they were in town now, and had the time, they just drove straight over to the Paradise Bar and went in. And whereas Harold had in the beginning been merely bored by it all, even given a headache by the ceaseless swinging wail of the blues guitar, and blistered lips from the barbecue so dredged in red pepper that it brought both tears and sweat to his face, he had finally come to enjoy these interludes at the Paradise, or rather to take them for granted — sentiments interchangeable in a boy of twelve.

"Well, who is it now? Seth Stevens's boy?"

Sitting on a stool next to the wall near where Harold stood was a blind black man of seventy or eighty, strumming a guitar in his lap, as he turned his face, smiling, toward Harold at the sound of his voice, asking, "Who is it now? Seth Stevens's boy?" and in his upturned face there

was such a soft unearthly radiance as could have been startling — a wide extraordinarily open face, and the expanse
of closed lids made it appear even more so, a face that when
singing would sometimes contort as though in pain or anger, and yet when turning to inquire, as in waiting for the
word, was lifted, smiling . . . even in the way an ordinary
man may cock his head to one side with a smile, this blind
man would, but tilting his chin as well, so that with the
light falling directly on his upturned face it seemed almost
to be illuminated.

"Who is it then? Hal Stevens?"

"Yeah, it's me, Tom," said the boy, laconic and restless
— accepting, yet uncertain it wasn't all a waste of time. He
sat down with his Dr Pepper in an old straight chair next
to the stool.

"How you doin', Blind Tom?" Asking this mostly out
of politeness, while the old blind man continued to smile
upward.

"You voice begin to change, Hal — I weren't right sure
it was you. How's your gran'daddy?"

"Aw he's awright. He's slowed down a lot though, I
guess."

Blind Tom always spoke as though Harold's grandfather
were still running their farm. It was something that Harold
had attempted to explain once, and that Tom had seemed
to understand, though gradually now the old notion had
stolen back into his talk, and Harold no longer tried to dis-
pel it.

"What kinda cotton you all got out there this year, Hal?"

"Aw I reckon it's pretty good — if the dang boll weevil
don't git at it again."

"What, he have some trouble with the weevil?"

"Aw, they got into that south quarter. We had to spray it over."

"Well, you gran'daddy ain't lose no cotton crop to the boll weevil, I tell you that!"

"Naw, we done sprayed it over now."

"He git good hands out there now?"

"Aw they say they ain't as good as they used to be — you know how they always say that."

"I use to pick-a-bale-a-day. I pick seben-hunnert twenty-three pounds one day, dry-load. He was down to the wagon hisself to see it weighed out. He tell you. They say it ain't never been beat in the county."

Harold nodded. "I know it, Tom."

An hour later, and the place was jumping — funky wailing blues and high wild laughter. Harold saw C.K., head back, eyes half-closed, smiling as he swayed to the music, a bottle of Sweet Lucy in one hand, and two dice in the other.

"Smart nigger double his money *quick*," he said suddenly, shaking the dice, next to his ear, "if he think ah ain't comin' out on . . . *wham*," and he threw the dice over the floor and against the bar, ". . . *SEBEN!*" Then he lay his head back laughing and tilted the bottle of wine.

"Crow suck that Lucy like it a big stick of tea!" said someone with a high-pitched laugh.

"He suck it like somethin' else ah think of too! Hee-hee. Gimme a taste of that Lucy, boy!"

"You all wise do you celebratin' *'foah* you puts you money down," said C.K., " 'cause you sho' gonna be cryin' the blues *after!* Where them dice?"

Old Wesley leaned behind the bar, picking his teeth with a matchstick. "Drink of this establishment not good enough for you, C.K., that you got to bring your own bottle in heah?"

"Never mind that, my man," said C.K., wiping his mouth. "You establishment don't carry drink of this particular quality." He slapped a quarter on the bar. "Gimme a glass."

Old Wesley put a large water glass on the bar. "And how 'bout you young frien' over there?" he asked, with a nod of mock severity at Harold.

"An my young frien' there have a Doctuh Peppah," said C.K., looking around at Harold as though he might have forgotten about him. "Ain't that right, Hal?"

"Naw, I still got one," said Harold sounding sullen and remote.

"Then you be awright," said C.K., and he tilted the bottle and watched the red wine tumble into his glass, a weary smile on his lips.

"Big Nail back," said Old Wesley.

"Is *that* a fack?" C.K. exclaimed, with a look of such astonished delight that one would surely know it was false.

"Sho'," said Wesley, jerking his head toward the end of the bar. "He done ast about you. See wheah he settin' ovah yondah?"

"Well, so he is," said C.K., partly turning around. "Ah swear ah never seen him when ah come in." But he said it in such a laughing way, taking a big drink at the same time, that it was apparent he had. "He lookin' fit, ain't he?" He laughed softly. "Ole Big Nail," he said, shaking his head as he turned back around. He refilled his half-full glass. "Ah likes to keep a full glass before me," he explained to Wesley, "at all time." He did a little dance-step then, holding on to the bar and looking down at his feet. "How's business with you, Mistuh Wesley?" he asked, returning to his drink.

" 'Bout the same as usual, ah reckon."

"Oh? Ah would of said it was pickin' up a mite," said C.K. smiling, looking at Big Nail — who glared back unblinking.

"An it remind me of a ver' funny story. These two boys from down Houston way was ovah in Paris, France, with the army you unnerstan', an' one day they was standin' on the corner without much in partic'lar to do, when a couple of o-fay chicks come strollin' by, you know what ah mean, a couple of nice li'l French gals — and they was ver' nice indeed, with the exception that one of them appeared to be considerable *older* than the other one, like she might be the great-granmutha of the other one or somethin' like that, you see. So these boys was diggin' these chicks, and one of them say: 'Man, let's make a move, ah believe we do awright there!' And the other one say: 'Well, now, similar thought occurred to me as well, but . . . er . . . uh . . . how is we goin' decide who take the *granmutha*? Ah don't want no old bitch like that!' So the other one say: 'How we decide? Why man, *ah* goin' take the granmutha! Ah the one see these chicks first, and ah gits to take my choice!' So the other one say: 'Well, now you talkin'! You gits the granmutha, an' ah gits the young one — *awright!* But tell me this, my man — how come you wants that old lady, instead of that fine young gal?' So the other one say: 'Why, boy, don't you know? Ain't you with it? She been white . . . *lon-guh!*'"

Finishing the story, C.K. lowered his head, closed-eyed as though he were going to cry, and stamped his foot, laughing.

Some of the people nearest him laughed too, but Old Wesley just shook his head. "You done tole that story two three time, C.K. Ain't you got no new story tell?"

C.K. sighed and refilled his glass. He took a big swig, swishing it around before he swallowed it. "Play the blues, Blind Tom," he said. "Play the blues one time." But Blind Tom was playing a jump-tune; he was shouting it:

> "My gal don't go fuh smokin'
> Likker jest make her flinch
> Seem she don't go fuh nothin'
> Ex-cept my big ten-inch . . .
> Record of de ban' dat play de blues.
> Ban' dat play de blues
> She jest loves
> My big ten-inch
> Record of her favo-rite blues.

> "Las' night ah try to tease her
> Ah give her a little pinch
> She say, 'Now stop dat jivin'
> An' git out yoah big ten-inch . . .
> Record of de ban' dat play de blues,
> Ban' dat play de blues.
> She jest love
> My big ten-inch
> Record of our favo-rite blues . . .'"

"Mind me ah hear a funny story today," said C.K., somewhat louder than before, and half turning away from the bar; then he stopped to laugh, closing his eyes and lowering his chin down to his chest, shaking his head as though trying not to laugh at all.

"Oh yeah, it were ver' funny."

Although his manner was loose and uninhibited, it suggested a certain restraint too, and an almost imperceptible half-smile, as of modesty, even as if he himself were quite objectively aware of how very good a story it was.

"These two boys was talkin', you see, and one of 'em say, he say: 'Well, boy, what you gonna do now you is *equal?*' And the other one say: 'Well now ah glad you ast me that, ah tell you what ah gonna do now ah's equal! Ah gonna git me one of them big . . . white . . . suits . . . and white tie, and white shoes and socks, and ah gonna buy me a white Cadillac, and then ah gonna drive down to Houston and git me a white woman!' And when he say that, the othah one jest laugh! So he say, salty-like, he say: 'What's the matter wif you, boy, you laugh like that when ah tell you my plan? You so smart, you tell me what *you* gonna do now you is equal!' So the second one say: 'Well, now ah tell you what *ah* gonna do now ah's equal! Ah gonna git me a black suit, and black shirt and tie, and black shoes and socks, and ah gonna buy me a black Cadillac, and then ah gonna drive down to Houston . . . and watch dem hang yoah equal black ass.' "

Though everyone had heard the story before, they almost all laughed, because of C.K.'s manner of telling it, the mock way he frowned and grimaced, and the short explosive way he delivered the "now-you-is-*equal*" refrain, making it nearly unintelligible.

"Ah think I know what he tryin' to say," said Big Nail, to no one in particular, holding a pair of dice by his ear, shaking them softly, "ah jest wondah why he don't put his money . . . where his big mouf is!" And he threw the dice, saying: "Hot . . . *seben!*"

So the game was joined, while on the stool against the wall where Harold sat, Blind Tom Ransom played the blues — and as the crap-game got under way, his head was lifted, sightless eyes seeming to range out over the players, singing:

"If you evah go to Fut Wurth
Boy you bettah ack right
You bettah not ar-gy
An' you bettah not fight!

"Shruf Tomlin of Fut Wurth
Cays a foaty-fouh gun
If you evah see 'im comin'
Well it too late to run!

" 'Cause he like to shoot rab-bit
Like to shoot 'em on de run
Seen dat Shruf hit a rab-bit
Wif his foaty-fouh gun!"

Someone encouraged him: "*Tell* it, Blind Tom!"

"An' he like to shoot de spar-ry
An' he like to shoot de quail
An' dere ain't many nig-ger
In de Fut Wurth jail!"

"Goddam, sing it, Blind Tom!"
And in a high wailing crescendo:

*"Yes he like to shoot de spar-ry
An' he like to shoot de quail!
An' dere ain't many nig-ger
In de Fut Wurth jail!"*

The crap-game progressed through the afternoon; by four o'clock there were about fifteen shooters. Harold had seen

C.K. cleaned out three times, and each time leave the bar, to come back a few minutes later with a new stake. The last time, though, he had come back with only another thirty-nine-cent bottle of Lucy.

"Put this bottle aside for me, my man," he said to Wesley, "till ah call for it later, in the cool of the evenin'."

"Who's winnin'?" asked Old Wesley.

"Ah wouldn't know nothin' 'bout that aspect of the game, ah assure you," said C.K.

"Big Nail winnin'!" said a boy about Harold's age who was picking cigarette butts off the floor by the bar. "Big Nail hot as a two-dollah pistol!"

C.K. gave a derisive snort and wiped his mouth. "Ah jest wish ah had me a stake," he said. "Now ah can *feel* it! Lemme have two-dollah, Mistah Wesley, ah give it to you first thing in the mornin' — on my way to work! Ah ain't kiddin' you!"

"Where you workin' now, C.K.?" asked Wesley, winking at Harold.

"Ah ain't *kid* you," C.K. said crossly, but then he sighed and turned away.

"Man, ah can sure feel it now!"

He started snapping his fingers, staring at his hand, fascinated. "Ump!" He made a couple of flourishes, and his shoulders hunched up and down in quick jerks, as though because of spasms outside his control. "Ump! Man, ah hot now, ah jest had me a goddam stake!"

"Here you is, boy."

The two bills, wadded together and soft with sweat, landed beside C.K.'s glass. He stared at them without looking up.

"Enjoy yourself," said Big Nail, who was standing next

to him and appeared to be absorbed in counting and arranging his money, a great deal of it.

C.K. picked up the crumpled notes and slowly straightened them out. "Shee-iit," he said, and then walked over to the game, taking his bottle with him.

Blind Tom was singing:

> "De longest tra-in
> Ah evah did see
> Was one hun-red coaches long . . ."

Back in the game, C.K. waited for the dice, ignoring the side bets.

"Ah only put my money on a sure thing this time of day," he said.

"Here old Crow tryin' to make his comeback!"

"What you shootin', C.K.?"

"Two-dollah? My, my, how the mighty have fallen!"

"You jest git in on that, boy," said C.K. "You be havin' all you want in a ver' short time!"

He rattled the dice, soft and then loud, he rolled them between his palms like pieces of putty — he blew on them, spit on them, rubbed them against his crotch, he raged at them like a sadistic lover: *Come*, you bitch, you hot mutha — hit 'em with it . . . *seben!*"

He made five straight passes without touching the money, and across the room Blind Tom was singing:

> "An de only gal
> Ah evah did love
> Was on dat tra-in
> An' gone . . ."

"What you shootin' *now*, C.K.?"

"You lookin' at it, daddy."

The two dollars, doubled five times, was now over sixty — and mostly in ones, it lay scattered between them like some kind of exotic garbage.

During the delay for getting the bet covered, because no one wanted to fade him any more, C.K. kept whispering to the dice and shaking them.

"They tryin' to cool you off, hot dice, they's so afraid, they tryin' to cool you off, you so hot! Lawd, ah feel you burn my hand, you so hot!

"Take all or any of it, boys," said C.K. "Goddam, step back, ah'm comin' out!"

"Come on out then," said Big Nail, standing behind the first row of the players crouched around the money, ". . . with all of it." And the bills fluttered down like big wet leaves.

"Shee-iit," said C.K., not looking up, shaking the dice slowly, "you hear that, dice? Ugly ole scarface man put down his money see you natural seben . . . yeah, ole scarface man pay see you natural seben . . . yeah, he want to see your big seben, baby," and he shook the dice gradually, and gradually faster now, near his head, rhythmically, as though he were playing a maraca or a tambourine, and he was humming along with the sound, saying, "yeah, now you talkin', baby, now you gittin' it . . . yeah . . . yeah . . . now we comin' out, dice, gonna show 'im the seben, gonna show 'im the 'leben," and as he talked to the dice, his voice rose and his tone gained command until, as the dice struck the wall, he was snarling, "*Hit him you mutha-fuckin'* SEBEN!"

Two aces.

Most were relieved that C.K.'s run was broken.

"Don't look too much like no seben to me," said someone

dryly. "Look more like the eyes of . . . of some kind of evil serpent!"

"Hee-hee! That's what it look like to me too," said another, who then called out: "Turn up the light, Mister Wesley — way it is now C.K.'s natural seben done look like ole snake-eyes!"

"You have to turn off de light 'fore that ever goin' *re*-semble a seben!"

"Hee-hee! You turn 'em off, them snake-eyes still *be* there! Gleamin' in the dark!"

Big Nail, on his knees, slowly gathered in the money, pulling it toward him, half folding, half wadding, stuffing it into his pockets, and then he stood up.

C.K. was standing too, his glass of Lucy in one hand, gazing at the floor, shaking his head in wonder at his loss.

Big Nail looked at him once again — eyes flat and dull as a rattler's.

"You ain't change much — is you, boy?" he finally said.

C.K. had a sip, turned the glass in his hand, regarding it in an apparent look of appraisal.

"Well, ah don't know," he said softly. "They's some people say ah ain't — then they's some say ah *is* — 'cause they say ah jest a little *faster* than ah use to be."

Big Nail frowned in an odd way. "Now ah jest wonder what do they mean by that, these people tellin' you that you so much faster than you use to be . . ."

"Oh they didn't say 'so much faster,' they jest say 'a little faster' — 'cause ah was *always* pretty fast . . . you may recall."

Big Nail finished his drink.

"Ah don't think ah follow their meanin'," he said. "Ah wonder do they mean fast like *that*," and as he said the word, he brought his glass quickly forward against the edge of the bar, then held it, very steady, turning it slowly and regarding it, the base still firm in his hand, the edges all jagged.

Neither of them looked up at the other, and after a few seconds, Big Nail lowered the glass to the bar.

"Well, no," said C.K., "ah would imagine — though, believe me, this is only a guess — that they was thinkin' more along different lines," and when he spoke, he gradually faced around to Big Nail, "ah would imagine they was thinkin' more along . . . *smooth-cuttin'* lines," and he described a wavering circle in front of him, his hand moving from his own unbroken glass toward his chest and suddenly sweeping down to his coat pocket and out with the razor — which he held then, open and poised, near his face, letting it glitter in the light, he who smiled now and looked directly into Big Nail's eyes for the first time that day. But Big Nail had moved too — had taken a step back, and he as well was holding his straight-edged razor there, just so, between two fingers and a thumb, like a barber. Smiling.

People suddenly began leaving the bar. The crap-game broke up. Harold watched them in openmouthed amazement. Old Wesley came around the end of the bar nearest the door. "They ain't goin' be none of that in here!" he said grimly, holding a half-taped chisel in his hand. "You got difference, git on outside, settle you difference out there!" He stood holding the chisel uncertainly.

"You stay out of this, old man," said Big Nail, backing out into the center of the room, "we jest havin' us a talk here."

Harold stood up. "C.K. . . . ," he said, tentative and unheard.

Besides Old Wesley, Harold, and Blind Tom Ransom,

there were only four other people in the bar now, and they were all carefully edging their way along the wall to the door. Outside, standing around the door and looking through the glass front of the bar, were about twenty-five people.

"Ain't that right, C.K.?"

Ssst-sst! Big Nail's razor made a hissing arc that touched C.K. just along the left side of his coat, and part of it fell away.

"That's right," said C.K., "we jest havin' us a friendly conversation." *Ssst-sst!* "Big Nail tellin' me how glad he be to git back home." *Ssst-sst!*

"Lawd God!" said someone.

"You stop it now!" said Wesley.

Outside, a woman screamed and started wailing, and one or two children began to cry.

"Mister Wesley," Harold implored, "please stop 'em . . ."

"Somebody call the po-lice!"

They circled each other like cats, now in one direction, now in the other, feinting steps forward and to the side, suddenly lashing out with the five-inch blades, and all the time smiling and talking with a grotesque gentility.

"You lookin' fit, C.K."

Ssst-sst!

"Well, thank you, Big Nail." *Ssst-sst!* "Ah was about to remark the same of you. Where you git that fancy white-man watch you wearin'?"

"You got to stop it now!" shouted Old Wesley. "We done call the po-lice!"

"Somebody git a gun!"

But they weren't listening anymore, only occasionally

pausing to wipe the blood from their eyes, moving slower now, even sagging a little, and they had stopped talking. Once they almost stopped moving altogether, standing about seven feet apart, their arms lower than before, each dripping blood like water from a rain-drenched shirt — and it seemed at that moment that they could both collapse.

"Well," said Big Nail, breathing with effort, "reckon we jest as soon . . . do it up right."

C.K. nodded slowly. "Reckon so . . . ," he said softly.

So they came together in the center of the room, for one last time, still smiling, and cut each other to ribbons.

Blind Tom Ransom, sitting on a stool inside the door, only heard it, a kind of scuffling, whistling sound, followed by a heavy swaying sigh. And he heard the clackety noise, as the razors dropped to the floor — first one, then the other — and finally the great sack-weight sound of the two men coming down, like monuments.

"It's all ovah now," Tom said, "all ovah now."

But, except for Harold, there was no one to hear him; the others had all turned away from it toward the end. And they didn't come back — only Old Wesley, to stand by the bar, his hands on his hips, shaking his head. He looked at Harold.

"Boy, you bettah git on home now," he said gently.

But before Harold could leave, a patrol car slid up in front of the place, and Old Wesley directed the boy in through a curtained door behind the bar, as two tall white men in wide-brimmed hats got out of the car, slamming the doors, and came inside.

"What the hell's goin' on here, Wesley?" asked one of

them, looking irately around the room and at the two bodies on the floor.

"Nothin' goin' on now, Officer," said Wesley, ". . . them two got into argyment . . . there weren't no trouble otherwise."

"How you doin', Blind Tom?" asked the second policeman.

"Awright, suh . . . who is it? Mistuh Bud Dawson?"

The first had gone over to the bodies.

"Put on some more light, Wesley . . . darker'n a well-digger's asshole in here — no wonder you have so much goddam trouble."

He turned one of the men over and put his flashlight on him.

"Goddam, they sure did it up right, didn't they?"

The other came over and gave a low whistle, frowning down at the bodies.

"Boy, I reckon they did," he said.

"You know 'em, Wesley?"

"Yessuh, I knows 'em."

One of the policemen crossed to the bar and took a small notebook out of his shirt pocket. The other one got himself a beer, then went back out and sat in the patrol car.

The policeman at the bar looked up at the ceiling.

"You still ain't got no more light in here than that?"

"Nosuh, waitin' for my fixtures."

The policeman gave a humorless laugh as he looked for a blank page in the notebook.

"You been waitin' a *long* time now for them fixtures, ain't you, Wesley?"

"Yessuh."

"Okay, what's their names?"

"One of 'em name C.K. Crow . . . and the other —"

"Wait a minute. 'C.K. Crow.' Any ad-dress?"

"Why ah don't rightly know they ad-dress. Ah think C.K. work and live out on the old Seth Stevens place, out near Indian River."

"You know how old he was?"

"C.K.? Why, he was thuty-five, thuty-six year old, ah guess."

"How 'bout the other one?"

"His name Emmett — everbody call him Big Nail."

"Emmett what?"

"Emmett Crow."

"They both named Crow?"

"Yessuh, that's right."

"What was they? Brothers?"

"Yessuh, that's right."

"Well, how old was he then?"

"Why ah don't rightly know now which one of them was the oldest of the two. They was always sayin' they was a *year older* than the other one, each of 'em say that, that he a year older. Then Big Nail, Emmett, he was away, you see, up nawth — in Chicago or New York City, believe it was . . . but they was both thuty-five, thuty-six year old."

The policeman closed his book and put it in his pocket.

"They got any folks here?"

Old Wesley nodded. "We'll look after 'em awright."

The policeman stood staring at the bodies for a minute.

"What was they fightin' about?"

"Why now ah don't rightly know. They got into argyment, you see . . . between themself. Wodn't nobody could stop it."

"What were they doin', shootin' craps?"

"Well, ah wouldn't know nothin' 'bout that! Ah tell you *one* thing, they sho' weren't shootin' no crap in here, ah know that much!"

The policeman stopped at the door, and looked down at Tom.

"Don't reckon *you* seen anything out of the ordinary goin' on lately, did you, Blind Tom?"

Blind Tom laughed.

"Nosuh, ah cain't say ah have."

"You gonna gimme a *re*-port on it though if you do see something out of the ordinary, ain't you, Blind Tom?"

"Why sho' ah is, Mistuh Bud Dawson, you knows that ah is! Fust unusual thing ah see, why ah be down to de station an' give a re-port, in full!"

They both laughed, and the policeman patted Blind Tom on the shoulder and left.

When the car had pulled away, Harold came out of the room behind the curtain, and people began coming back into the bar.

Blind Tom was singing the blues.

"Ah jest wonder how C.K. feel," said someone, "if he know he gonna be buried on Big Nail's money. I bet he wouldn't like it!"

Old Wesley frowned. "C.K. 'preciate a good send-off as well as the next man. Besides," he added, "C.K. weren't never one to hold a grudge for ver' long." He looked at Harold, ashen and devastated with shock.

"Ain't that right, boy?"

XV

I CAN'T LISTEN to it again," said Harold's mother, walking past the kitchen table, one hand raised to her head. "You'll have to tell him yourself. I'll tell your granddad, there's no use in him hearing it the way you tell it. But you'll have to tell your daddy."

"Well, that's the way it happened, dang it," said Harold, frowning down at the empty plate in front of him.

"Well, I don't care, I don't want to hear it. Now you tell him and then you go wash. We're goin' to have supper in a few minutes."

She walked out of the room and left Harold sitting alone at the table. Outside the dogs were barking, and he heard his father on the porch, stamping his feet, kicking the mud from his shoes; then the door opened and he came inside, still stamping his feet as though it were winter. He leaned the shotgun against the wall under a rack of others.

"I want you to clean that gun after supper, Son," he said. "Where's your mother?"

"She's upstairs."

"Looka here, boy," said his father, smiling now, holding up a brace of fat bobwhite quail, "ain't them good 'uns?"

"C.K.'s dead, Dad," said Harold, just as he had planned, as gravely as he could, not feeling anything except trying to measure up to the adult type of seriousness he believed the words must have.

"What're you talkin' about, Son?" demanded his father, scowling in anger and impatience. "Didn't you and him pick up that feed?" He stamped over to the sink and laid the birds down there to turn and face the boy and have it out. "Now what're you talkin' about?"

And for Harold it was only then, with the moment of his father's disbelief, that the reality of it cut through his shock and fell across his heart like a knife. Something jumped and caught inside his throat and knotted behind his eyes. He looked down at the table, shaking his head, and then the thing inside his throat, burning behind his eyes, broke loose, in a short terrible burst, and he stiffly raised one arm to his face to try and choke away the terrible sobs, and the incredible tears — not the kind of tears he had known before, but tears of the first bewildering sorrow.

His father said nothing, frowning in consternation; then he came over and stood by him, and finally put one hand gently, awkwardly, on his shoulder.

At the supper table, no more was said about it, until once when Harold's father sat for a moment gazing distraitly at the knife in his hand. "Damn niggers," he said softly, "what did they git into a fight about anyway?"

"Drink some milk, Son," said his mother, raising the big pitcher, "you've got to have something."

"What was it they was fightin' about?" repeated his father.

Harold dumbly watched the glass in his hand, the white milk tumbling in. He pushed the glass away.

"Aw, I dunno," he said stiffly, "they got into argument — about one thing and another, and then they got to fightin' — wasn't nobody could stop it."

"Hadn't been a-shootin' crap?" said his old grandfather, brooding forward over his plate toward the boy like a hawk.

"No sir," said Harold, "they weren't doin' nothin' like that."

The old man grunted and kept on eating.

XVI

IN the open-end dirt-floor shed, Harold sat in the same place where C.K. used to read his *Western Story*. With the .22 rifle raised to his shoulder, he fired shot after shot into a paper target about fifteen feet away. He fired until the bull's-eye was completely shot away, and in its place only a ragged hole. But he continued shooting until the gun was empty.

He was sitting cross-legged, the shell-box and fruit-jar of grass at his feet. Using the knife that had skinned the rabbit and scooping with his hands, he dug a hole in the soft earth and put the two containers in it and covered them over. He gazed down for a long moment at the place where they were hidden. He knew they were buried deep enough not to be discovered, but not so deep that he couldn't get to them, if he should ever want to.